Temptations of Christmas Future

A Christmas Carol

Book 3

Temptations of Christmas Future

A Christmas Carol

Book 3

BY

LEXI POST

Temptations of Christmas Future:

A Christmas Carol, Book 3 Summary

Thanks to his shock tactics and pessimistic attitude, Scottish spirit guide Malcolm MacLachlan's job is on the line. What else did they expect from a former Glasgow Watchman? For his final assignment, he chooses his partner based on the probability of success, and Joy Collingwood is the very best. That he can prove to her the future isn't all puppies and marshmallows is an added bonus.

Joy is thrilled to help Malcolm, but their different methods threaten the success of their collaboration. If they can't find some common ground, they'll fail. What she doesn't expect is that their common ground will be her bed and her deepest secret will be revealed.

Yet her secrets are nothing compared to Malcolm's and their revelation could jeopardize everything…including her heart.

For updates, sneak peeks, and special prizes, sign up to receive the latest news from Lexi Post at http://bit.ly/LexiUpdate

Acknowledgments

For Bob Fabich, Sr., my very own Christmas temptation. And for my sister Paige Wood, who I love spending Christmas with and who helps my stories shine.

Thank you to my daughter-in-law Rebecca Curran Fabich who answered all my questions on words, food, customs and everything else in regards to her home country of Scotland. A special thank you to Elizabeth Mair of Darvel, Scotland, a good friend who is always willing to share some of the details of life in town.

Once again, I must thank my amazing critique partner, Marie Patrick, who reads my pages as fast as I can write them. Believe me, they are so much better for her insight.

And I can't close without thanking my pre-pub team, Sarah Fisher and Lisa Fishback. You ladies make my stories look so much better.

Author's Note

Temptations of Christmas Future was inspired by *A Christmas Carol* by Charles Dickens. In Dickens' story, Ebenezer Scrooge, a miserly curmudgeon, is told by the spirit of his former business partner, Marley, that he will be visited by three ghosts and if he doesn't change his ways he will pay for it in the afterlife. Scrooge scoffs at the idea but as he journeys into his past, present, and future with the spirit of each period of his life, he sees the error of his ways and becomes a completely different man when he wakes up on Christmas day.

But what if the spirit itself, as well as the living human, was in need of help, and the visit could make a difference in the existence of both? Could the Spirits of Christmas Future come to terms with their former lives while helping a young widow grow and her late husband succeed? Do any of them really have control of their futures or is fate in charge? And most importantly, can love conquer all even in the afterlife?

Chapter One

Oh, yes." Joy gripped the satin sheets as pleasure shot from the juncture of her thighs to her very fingertips. The man lapping at her clit knew what he was doing, his rhythm, with the toy moving in and out of her sheath, was the perfect pace.

When his free hand moved up to cup her breast, she held her breath knowing what would come next.

He didn't disappoint. His fingers moved around to her hard nipple to roll and pinch it, sending her over the edge into her climax.

She arched upward, her body on fire, consumed by an ecstasy only he could give her. Her peak of pleasure continued, his mouth an instrument of erotic torture, refusing to release her.

She quivered as he held her there, at her pinnacle, her throat dry from panting, her body strung taught with wave after wave of bliss sweeping through her.

Finally, he removed the toy, as well as his hand from her breast to spread her legs wider. His tongue traveled down to her opening to lick the juices of her orgasm, the scruff on his face sending tingles of sensation across her inner thighs. His need for her taste gave her a chance to relax and revel in her contentment.

She lightly grasped his head beneath the hooded cape he always wore, the strands of his silky black hair wrapping around her fingers almost as if they had a mind of their own, their sensuality as captivating as the rest of him. He was a master in the art of sexual stimuli.

Frowning, she tried to remember his name. Why couldn't she remember his name? He always gave her such perfect pleasure. She looked down but the hood obscured his face. She wanted to see him, remember who he was.

She tugged on his hair to have him lift his head. His dark eyes bored into her with a carnal knowledge far deeper than her own. As his full face came into view, he licked his sensual lips, one side quirking upward just slightly.

"Malcolm."

She let her hands go lax, not wanting him any closer, but he continued to rise, pulling himself over her, his gaze holding her immobile. His face lowered, his lips touched hers, and as he breached her mouth with his tongue to share her taste, his cock speared her to its hilt.

Joy sat up in bed, her heart racing as the dream remained in her consciousness to titillate her with details. She moaned, closing her eyes again before snapping them open once more as Malcolm's visage floated beneath her eyelids.

Throwing her legs over the side of her bed, she ran her hands through her auburn hair. She was a mess. Her body overheated and sweating, her hair tangled, and her thighs wet from her too satisfying dream. Too bad her psyche wasn't equally satisfied.

She padded across the marble floor and into her bathroom. The air in the replica of her Scottsdale home was cool against her damp skin. Turning on the water in the glass and stone shower, she waited for it to warm.

It took less than three seconds before she was able to stand under the spray. One of the perks of the afterlife was the elimination of tiny inconveniences. The water soaked her hair, and she squirted her favorite body wash into her palm.

"Hmmm." The peppermint scent lifted her spirits and pushed away her disturbing dream. She knew exactly why she had it. Every time she ran into Malcolm MacLachlan, he burrowed into her subconscious. Not that her consciousness was immune to him either. No woman, living or dead, could be oblivious to him.

That spirit guide had a body that would send even the most sexual woman into a faint. He didn't exactly flaunt it, his dark brown hooded cape covering him most of the time, like a druid of old, but when he turned a certain way—

She pulled her hand from between her thighs and washed her legs. Luckily, he rarely visited any of the spirit guide gathering areas. She just happened to have literally bumped into him in the hallway outside their supervisor's door yesterday as she'd exited, his evergreen scent bringing to mind dark forests and even darker orgies.

Cameron had been very pleased with her work on her last assignment. He even told her she could take a few days to play. Personally, she thought her supervisor seemed a little distracted.

They all knew he'd been sending spirit guides to help his wife move on after his death. That in itself was usually not allowed. Checking on family members after a spirit guide's death was an absolute no-no. She couldn't even visit her niece, something she wished to do more than anything. To know her sacrifice had meant something would be very reassuring.

Squeezing out a few squirts of shampoo, she massaged it into her hair, the candy cane aroma of it soothing her despite her growing concern. Coco and Ian, the last two spirits to be assigned to Cameron's wife never returned. Coco had been her friend for a long time and whenever they had time to play, they'd done it together.

When she asked Cameron where Coco was, he just said she was no longer a spirit guide. She'd tried to push the issue, but he scowled at her and the rumors about his mental stability had her closing her mouth. She felt sorry for him. He had a lot of pressure from above.

Rinsing her hair, she tried to focus on what to do with her free time. Though there was no such thing as time in the afterlife, they all sensed it as they had in life, so some time away from helping the living was always welcome.

Finished with her shower, she waved her hand and it stopped.

She dried herself and donned her turquoise satin robe. "My coffee." A cup of coffee appeared on the sink next to her. Taking a sip, she looked in the mirror. "Make up." She'd just taken the cup away when her face was enhanced with just the right amount of color. She may be dead, but that didn't mean she should get lazy.

Taking her cup with her, she meandered over to her walk-in closet to review her clothes. She phased before speaking. "I think my purple and turquoise sundress will do." Instantly, she had the sleeveless dress on. She returned to being solid again. She could have stayed solid and simply put on her clothes herself, but there were certain advantages to phasing like instantly being dressed or traveling through space and time.

She took another sip of coffee. She preferred her solid state as did most spirit guides since that was what they were used to. Besides, eating was much more enjoyable while solid.

A buzzer on her counter lit just before her supervisor's voice came through. "Joy, could you come to my office, please?" Though Cameron asked, it wasn't really a question.

"Of course." She didn't wait for an answer. Phasing, she quickly floated through her ceiling.

~~*~~

Malcolm grinned in the face of his boss's frown. He'd surprised the man to speechlessness before the arguing began. What did he care? He had nothing to lose. Since this would be his last assignment, he might as well prove his point in the process.

Cameron Douglas moved his thick brown hair off his forehead. "Are you sure you want Joy for a partner? I can think of a dozen other spirit guides that might be of more help to you. As I said, this is your last chance. I'd think you'd want someone you could work well with."

"If you think someone else would be better then why let me choose who I want?" He floated closer and solidified. "If I choose poorly then I fail and I'm out of your hair. I can't believe you want me to succeed. What game are you playing, Douglas?"

His supervisor turned away from him, his movements rigid. "Believe me, if I had a choice, you'd be the last one I'd send on this assignment."

He stiffened. His work had always produced the wanted results. If his methods were different from most spirit guides, what did it matter? He followed the rules and accomplished what needed to be done. If half of them, his boss included, had any inkling of what the future held, they'd change how they guided the living, of that he was sure.

Refusing to let Cameron know he was irritated, he leaned against the wall next to his boss's desk to await his partner. He couldn't imagine them reassigning him. It wasn't as if the afterlife needed to be protected, which was the only other skill he excelled at. Something wasn't making sense.

He was the only spirit guide left from the future. The rest were either reassigned or had disappeared. That he was being given a partner on this case meant it would be a particularly difficult one. Rarely did they partner up.

"If you didn't always show the worst-case scenario and if you would carefully couch your words in more palatable phrases, you wouldn't be in jeopardy of losing your position." Cameron's voice had just a tinge of desperation to it.

Something was seriously wrong. Though he'd never been overly fond of his boss, the man had a stellar track record and did his job with confidence. "Have I ever failed to deliver the desired outcome?"

Cameron sighed. "It's not just the outcome that counts. The process should also be—never mind. It's not worth having this conversation for the hundredth time." Cameron's shoulders slumped in defeat.

Now he was sure something, other than his own dismissal, was riding on this assignment. A twinge of guilt niggled at his psyche, but he pushed it away. Joy was an accomplished spirit guide. The antithesis of him, but still very successful. Not only would they do what needed to be done, but he would show her reality, proving to her that her way of looking at life and death was far too idealistic.

She was too happy and too confident in that happiness. She needed to be taught, as he'd taught a couple others, that her way of guiding the living would only leave them unprepared for what lay ahead. The future was not puppies and marshmallows.

Cameron leaned back in his chair and looked over at him. "How do you know Joy? I didn't think you spent your free time in the same places she does."

He shook his head. "I don't. But having been here longer than you, I run into other guides whether I want to or not. I also know of her success rate with the living, and if as you say, this is my last chance to prove I should keep my job, I want the best."

His boss nodded. "She is the best, but her methods are far different from yours. Then again, maybe you'll learn something that will help you. I'd listen to her if I were you."

Or maybe she'd learn from him, which was his goal. He crossed his arms, refusing to respond to Cameron's statement. The woman was unprepared for what he planned to—

Joy Collingwood phased through the ceiling and floated down to hover in front of Cameron's desk before turning solid. Her sleeveless dress cinched in at the waist to show off her figure and flared out slightly at the knee. The turquoise running riot through the purple swirls on the material matched her eyes perfectly, and knowing her, that was planned.

His gaze followed her long legs down to her feet where she wore strappy sandals and a practical heel. As his eyes moved to her face, he found her straight auburn hair swept up in a neat bun, as usual. She wore small pearl earrings in her pierced ears and a pearl necklace that matched the neckline of her modest dress. Despite that, his body still noticed every feminine curve from her ample breasts to her rounded hips.

The scent of peppermint wafted toward him, and he barely refrained from grimacing, the scent itself too happy for his tastes. As her lips lifted in a polite smile toward their boss, he found himself focused on her white teeth. She looked like an ad in one of those woman's magazines that were so popular in America in the twentieth century. As far as he was concerned, her entire appearance was unreal. Too perfect. Too put together. Too content.

He would change that.

"You wished to see me?" Even her voice was soothing, which caused irritation to flash through him.

Cameron rose from behind the desk and held out his hand. "Please take a seat."

She sat, crossing one long limb over the other before her gaze rested on him. "Oh, hello Malcolm."

He nodded once, but didn't say anything. Instead, he watched her like a hawk watched a hare.

She smiled politely, but it didn't quite reach her bright blue-green eyes. She returned her gaze to Cameron as if she wished to dismiss him. She was in for a surprise.

Cameron leaned against his desk. "I know I told you to take some time to relax after your last case, but I'm afraid the powers-that-be have other plans."

At his boss's phrasing, Malcolm perked up. He's the one who chose Joy to partner with, not the higher ups. Did that mean he was being tested by those above Cameron? If he was, did they know he'd choose Joy or would they be as surprised as Cameron to discover his choice? He didn't like being manipulated. It only happened once that he knew of when he was alive and it had cost him his life.

Again, a pang of conscience hit him for dragging Joy into his mission, but it left as soon as it arrived. If Cameron's boss expected him to fail, he or she or it was in for a rude awakening.

Joy nodded. "Of course, I understand. I hadn't decided what I wanted to do anyway." She cocked her head slightly to the right when she made her statement.

Something inside him suggested she hadn't been completely truthful. Not that she lied, but maybe didn't admit to everything. He'd have to watch that behavior on their assignment. He'd learned a lot on the streets that had kept him alive for as long as he was there.

Cameron looked over at him. "Would you mind coming over here so I can talk to you both at the same time?"

He pushed away from the wall and strode toward Joy, taking a stance behind her chair and to the right. This close, he could smell the sweet peppermint scent emanating from her. It reminded him of when he was a little boy. He'd loved candy canes back then, often eating them all off the tree before Christmas day.

The last thing he needed was to be reminded of his early years before he knew what awaited him in the world. "What is this assignment you have for us?"

"Us?" Joy turned around to look at him.

Was that merely surprise or fear he saw in her eyes? He couldn't be sure because she turned back to face Cameron.

Their supervisor nodded. "Yes, this is a difficult assignment, and I need two very good spirit guides on it."

Joy sat a little straighter at the compliment. "I'm happy to help."

He wanted to tell her Cameron was playing on her ego, but he kept silent, more interested in their task than in edifying his partner on the ways their boss manipulated spirit guides.

Cameron sighed deeply before glancing from him to Joy, but he kept his focus on her as he spoke. "Your assignment is my wife, Holly."

He chuckled, loving the irony of the importance of his last assignment to his boss, but he didn't miss Joy's complexion fading to a pasty white.

Cameron didn't notice as he turned his focus on him and scowled. "This is no laughing matter."

"You can't tell me you don't see the irony of this. If I'm not successful, not only am I a failure, but you are too. It forces you to want me to succeed. You actually have to hope you get to keep me around."

Cameron shook his head. "I hold nothing against you, Malcolm. If it was my choice, you'd continue for as long as I'm here. I'm not thrilled with your methods, but you do accomplish your goals."

His boss's unexpected endorsement both surprised him and made him more nervous. He knew how *Cameron* worked, but those who pulled the man's strings were a complete unknown. This was one time he wished he could see the future of those in the afterlife.

"What happened to Coco?" Joy's voice surprised them both.

Cameron stood and walked around his desk. "She has moved on."

That was as ambiguous an answer as any he'd heard in all his time as a spirit guide, and from the look on Joy's face, she recognized it for the brush off it was.

His boss continued. "Holly will be expecting you on Christmas Eve." He pushed a file across his desk. "Everything you need to know is in here, but…" The man stared at the packet of paper beneath his hand as if he wished he didn't have to let it go. "This is confidential. No discussing it with other guides or trainers or anyone except me."

Ah, the man's personal relationship to his wife was revealed inside. Malcolm couldn't wait to read it.

Joy leaned forward and with her long, polish-free nails pulled the file from Cameron's hand and set it on her lap. "What is our goal for Holly?" Her voice, which had been smooth as silk before, had a scratchy undertone now. She obviously knew more than he did about this assignment and from her serious face, it wasn't good.

Cameron smiled. "I need my wife to be open to expanding her horizons, deepening her connections to others."

"That's a bit broad. Anything or person in particular?" He didn't want to lose his position over semantics. He wanted specifics.

His boss leaned back in his chair and shook his head. "No, nothing in particular. It's more a mindset than anything else. She has accepted my death and begun to live, but only at the surface level. She stays within her comfort area, what she already knows, like our Christmas Shop and the Deervale community. I need her to be open to going beyond what she knows and feels now."

"So, you want her to start living her own life separate from you." Joy's face had relaxed, and she appeared a bit more confident.

Every person he'd ever known had no problem moving beyond a break up or divorce. He didn't see much difference with the death of a spouse. "What am I missing here? Why wouldn't she be doing that anyway? Why would you need two spirit guides for that?"

Both Cameron and Joy looked at him with wide eyes, before Cameron's mouth lowered into a frown. "Because my wife and I loved each other."

He opened his mouth to respond, but Joy interrupted him. "Malcolm, where have you been? Cameron and Holly were soulmates."

Schitz. Just his luck. He was far too familiar with the trouble with that.

~~*~~

Joy finished reading the file on Holly and carefully returned all the papers back in order. Rising from her kitchen table, she strolled into her living room where Malcolm waited.

Just having him in her space had super-charged her libido. She'd never been attracted to the bad boy type before. Maybe he wasn't a bad boy after all, not that she'd had any better luck with good boy types either. "Here you are." She held out the file.

He'd thrown back his hood, which in itself was new to her as he always wore it when she'd seen him before. His black glossy hair just begged her to run her hands through it. Instead, she was careful his hand didn't touch hers as he accepted the documents.

"Is it as bad as I think?" He looked up at her, his brown eyes searching hers for the truth.

"It depends on what you think is bad. Cameron and Holly have one of those love stories that lasts beyond death, which is wonderful and beautiful and —"

"And the worst-case scenario given our task." He slapped the file against his bare knee, his red, black and royal blue kilt having fallen open.

She forced her gaze from his dusky skin, her body already reacting to him. "Not necessarily. I'm sure if we put our heads together, we can come up with a workable strategy."

He lowered his dark brows and looked at her as if she were crazy. "Right. And while we're at it, let's develop a plan for world peace."

He didn't have to be an ass about it. "I'm sure one is being worked on even as we speak."

He grunted as he opened the file, his message clear. He thought her naïve. She should have known he'd be a jerk.

Turning, she headed back to her kitchen.

"Where are you going?"

His voice caused her to halt. "I thought I'd get us some iced tea while you read."

"Iced tea." He shook his head. "Add some Lapsir to that."

"Lapsir?" She'd never heard of that drink.

"It was invented after you transitioned. Just ask for it, and be liberal with it."

She continued to her kitchen. The rumors about Malcolm were true. He came from the future, or rather the future compared to most of the spirits. Time had no meaning in the afterlife, which is why she didn't mind getting another case. If she wanted to, she could go to a Tahiti replica and enjoy the warm waters for days and be back within seconds, but she wouldn't be able to relax knowing she would be working with Malcolm.

That and their assignment. She shivered.

Quickly, she pulled the iced tea out of her fridge and poured it into two glasses. "A bottle of Lapsir." The red liquid in the glass bottle that appeared seemed to move like fire, streaks of yellow and orange clearly inside it.

Instead of pouring it into Malcolm's glass, she put it on a tray and brought it back to the living room. She could have ordered it while there, but she wanted to give him a chance to read about Holly and Cameron while alone. It had brought tears to her eyes, though she doubted it would affect him in the same way.

He was waiting for her as she put the tray down on her glass coffee table. He sat on her gray and black blotch couch, his brown cape, dark complexion and black hair a handsome compliment to her furniture.

She took a seat on her zebra striped recliner as she lifted her glass from the tray. "I thought I'd let you pour your own Lapsir."

Opening the bottle, he didn't respond. He poured a significant amount into the tea, causing it to take on the colors of the liquor. After capping the bottle, he raised his glass. "To success."

She raised her glass as well before they both drank. "I think getting Holly to be open to living her own life will be difficult, but not impossible."

Malcolm looked at her and laughed. "You really *are* an optimist. This assignment, if we're successful, is going to wring us out and drop us in a heap on a stone-cold floor. However, if as I suspect, we fail, which I believe is the expectation, then we succeed in meeting their goals."

She felt her body grow cold as her throat tried to close. "We can't fail." Her words came out scratchy.

"Why? You had the same reaction when you found out Holly was our assignment. What do you know?"

It was more what she didn't know. "You read the whole file?"

He nodded.

He must have used the viewer, a reenactment of someone's life that never completely portrayed the nuances, in her opinion. "Every spirit guide pair that has visited Holly has disappeared."

He gave her a look of amused disbelief. "You don't know that."

"I do." She paused to take a deep breath to settle her nerves, her fear getting the better of her. "My friend Coco was assigned to be Holly's Spirit of Christmas Present along with Ian Fergusson. Neither has returned."

He appeared to give that some thought. "They could have been given another assignment."

This time *she* gave him a look of disbelief. "Both of them? You know as well as I do that Cameron only assigns paired spirit guides as an exception rather than as a rule. I tell you, they're gone." She pointed to the file he'd laid on the couch next to him. "Didn't you notice there was no mention of a debrief? We *always* debrief with Cameron."

"Say you're correct, and we are expected to fail and disappear. That leaves us only one option."

His confidence gave her hope. "What's that?"

"We must succeed."

Her hope fizzled and died. Of course she wanted to succeed, but it would be close to impossible unless Malcolm had some serious practical ideas.

Chapter Two

Malcolm floated next to Joy along the street of Deervale, his conscience getting the better of him. If he'd known they'd be set up to fail, he would never have chosen Joy. He still wanted to show her that the world wasn't as rosy and hopeful as she thought it to be, but he didn't want the responsibility, and guilt, of having been the one to cause her dismissal as a spirit guide, or worse, her disintegration all together. One woman on his conscience was enough.

He'd bet his cape that the higher-ups knew he'd choose Joy, though how could they when he'd never mentioned his goal to disillusion her to anyone? For all he knew, they invaded his head when he slept.

"Oh, look. Holly's entering the bakery. I wonder why? Usually Mrs. Bell bakes her a clootie dumpling for Christmas. Maybe Holly is having a party and needs more food."

Malcolm looked at the clear blue sky as if its soothing color could give him the willpower to stop from making fun of Joy. How important could Mrs. Bell be to Holly? "Why don't we follow her inside and find out what she's about?"

Joy nodded and headed into the building through the front window.

He preferred to scout out his assignment alone, but his gut told him their fates were now tied together, so he wanted to be sure they both remained cognizant of each other's findings. In life, he had rarely worked with a partner, but he'd found it was always smart to get another point of view, even if it was eventually dismissed.

The bakery was packed with people ordering sweets and breads for Christmas dinner. Though the holiday was still a week away, the happiness in the air was palpable. He tamped down his usual cynical comment. He would make allowances for the time of year. Even the Glasgow underbelly ramped up at the end of the year for Hogmanay.

"Oh look. She's placing an order. That must mean she's planning to go to Brody and Sarah's for their annual Christmas Eve party." Joy looked back at him. "Brody and Ethan were Cameron's best friends. Brody is the one just like him. Ethan is far more cautious."

"Aye. I viewed the file."

Joy's cheeks flushed. "I'm sorry. I'm not used to having a partner."

She turned back to watch, and he swallowed his response.

Holly made it to the low counter. Cameron's wife had a bit more meat on her bones than Joy with thick dark brown hair. When she smiled at the young woman behind the counter, her round face lit up and a dimple appeared on her right cheek. "Good afternoon, Miss Bryden. Could I order two mince pies please?"

The young woman with her wavy chestnut hair clipped on top of her head winked. "Two? Does that mean you have a couple parties to go to?"

Holly shook her head. "No, just one, Brody and Sarah's. But there will be a lot of people there. Are you going to any parties?"

Milly Bryden grinned. "I have five the week of Christmas."

"Oh wow, you're very popular."

The young woman finished punching the order into the register. "Not really. Just family and friends."

Holly handed her a credit card then returned it to her purse.

"Thank you. I'll be by on the twenty-third to pick them up." As she made her way through the crowd, a number of people chatted with her.

Malcolm didn't have to observe Holly Douglas very long to conclude that she and Joy would be kindred spirits. Her easy-going ways and quick smile told him that. Then again, with both of them liking Christmas and being from America, it would make it even harder for him.

Joy floated over. "She seems to have re-engaged in her community thanks to Coco and Ian."

He nodded to be polite, but his thoughts weren't on Holly. He wanted to discover what Cameron's bosses were hoping to achieve and then thwart them. If they planned to be rid of him and Joy like they were rid of Ian and Coco, he needed to focus more on that.

"Even Holly hiring an employee so she isn't stuck at the shop all day shows a willingness to change. Maybe our task won't be that hard after all." Joy smiled.

He rubbed his forehead at Joy's optimistic attitude to keep from snapping at her. "I believe the kind of change Cameron is referring to is more like a major life change, such as selling her Christmas Shop or adopting a child, or something of that magnitude."

Joy's happy smile fell. "I know that. I was simply pointing out that she has already made a small change, and I'll bet there are more that we can use to build on."

His partner didn't wait for a response, but floated out of the bakery to follow Holly. He was glad to see she had a little backbone. It meant he wouldn't have to tread too lightly. He wanted to change her attitude, not crush her.

He was about to leave the bakery as well when he noticed someone watching Holly leave through the window. He started to float in that direction when a loud crash caught his attention near the counter.

A young boy had knocked over the donut tree. He had a feeling the boy had attempted to steal a few donuts. That's how it all started. From donuts to grand theft. Turning back toward the window, he found the person gone.

His senses immediately went into alert mode. There was more afoot than normal with this case. He sped through time to Holly and Cameron's One of a Kind Christmas Shop where Joy was already observing.

Holly spoke to a customer near the fifteen-foot Christmas tree in the middle of the shop. "Did you have something in mind, Luca?"

The tall young man had a confidence about him that came with someone who had found the love of his life. Malcolm preferred to forget about that particular time in his own.

"I want something that will remind Milly of her grandmother. This will be her first Christmas without her."

"What a beautiful idea." Holly, now with a Santa hat covering the top of her head, her thick brown hair falling to her shoulders, looked pleased. "What were some of the things Milly and her grandmother did together?"

The young man grinned. "They made the best sugar cookies and my favorite, trifle."

Holly gave him a sly smile. "That sounds more like what you liked the most than what Milly may have liked."

Luca laughed. "You're right." The young man stared at the tree, but he obviously was thinking.

Malcolm smelled Joy's peppermint scent before she came up behind him. "I really like Cameron's wife. She's smart and intuitive. She's not interrupting Luca while he tries to think, though I'm sure she has a number of suggestions she can make."

"That could mean we'll move faster through her future scenarios."

"Don't you wish you could look into the future of your own life, to see how things played out after you were gone?"

"No." He already knew what happened after he was shot and stabbed and hung up like a trophy. The underground alleyways of Glasgow returned to the miscreants of a new generation.

Joy studied him, and he quickly turned away. She didn't need to see his life. It was better if he showed her where Holly might be headed instead. It was less traumatic.

"Oh, I know." Luca drew their attention again. "Granny and Milly spent the month before Burns Night making new lace handkerchiefs for family and friends to wear. Granny just loved pulling out that old loom and working with Milly. That was their special time alone. No one but Milly knows how to do that."

"That's perfect." Holly smiled. "Now to find something that will reflect that memory. I have a few ideas. Come over here."

Joy's gaze followed the two as they walked away toward a corner of the shop where shelves of laser cut wood ornaments were displayed. "I believe the file said Milly is Luca's soulmate, or rather one of them. I bet Holly had something to do with them meeting this year."

He'd agree if it actually mattered.

"I never did marry. Did you, Malcolm?"

Joy's question caught him off guard. "Why didn't you marry?"

She sighed. "I never found the right man. I thought I would be married at an early age and have a bevy of children, but being a hospice nurse limited my time to meet people. I mean people outside the family and friends of my patients." She cocked her head to the right.

Hospice? The word was no longer in use during his life. It took him a moment to pull up the meaning. "Were you always a hospice nurse or did you do other types of nursing?" He couldn't reconcile the poised, optimistic Joy with someone who worked around death all her life.

"Mostly. I had to work in different departments during my clinicals, but as soon as I graduated, I went right into hospice care."

"Why?" He couldn't help asking. He thought he'd be giving her a reality check when all along she'd worked with the dying? Something didn't fit.

"Why not? I was a nurse and nurses help people. I couldn't think of a better place than to help a patient die with dignity and grace. I also was able to help the families of my patients. It was a very rewarding career."

"Did you ever lose someone in your family? Someone close to you?"

She shook her head. "Not as an adult. I did lose my grandmother when I was young. I guess I had it easy. I was the first in my family to leave."

Now it made sense. The death and suffering she'd witnessed wasn't personal. Not that he expected it was easy, but it wasn't like having someone she loved killed in front of her eyes.

In that way, she was ignorant, and hopefully always would be. But it did explain why she was so positive. Helping patients die peacefully was one thing. Watching helplessly as someone he loved died in his arms was a completely different experience.

"Did you want to watch Holly some more, or should we return to Cameron and let him know we're ready? That is if you still agree on our course of action."

He nodded. He completely agreed, but he doubted she'd continue to once she realized what he planned for Holly to learn from the visits he chose. Holly already knew what keen loss was. They wouldn't be here now if she didn't. He had no doubt that she'd handle his visits to the future better than Joy would.

Opening Joy's eyes would put them at odds and help him ignore his appreciation of her physically. The last thing he'd ever do is become involved with a woman again, especially one as happy as Joy.

~~*~~

Holly locked the door behind Mr. Branson, happy to see he'd spent his usual half hour picking out just the right ornament. His wife must be paying attention to him again. Last year at Christmas, she'd tried making his wife jealous with a few anonymous phone calls, but the woman had been oblivious. As it turned out, in the spring Mr. Branson had a heart attack and that woke up Mrs. Branson to how close she'd come to losing him.

Luckily, the elderly man lived, and she was so pleased. His wife also realized in time how lucky she was. They celebrated their sixty-first anniversary at the Turnberry Golf Resort with many family and friends just last month.

Holly shook her head. Why did people not appreciate those in their lives while they had them? It shouldn't take a brush with death to focus on what was important. She'd always appreciated Cam every day of her life. Their time together was far too short.

At the thought that he would visit her in a matter of minutes, she hit the switch that turned off all the Christmas lights in their little store on Main Street. Lastly, she turned off the outside light that proclaimed it the One of a Kind Christmas Shop.

Ducking behind the tapestry that covered the door between the shop and their house, she stepped inside. She dropped her purse on the table next to the door and flicked on the light. "Mac?"

She frowned as she scanned the decorated living room. Some might say over-decorated, but it was perfect for her and Cam…and Mac. "Mac, where are you?"

Holy crap, did she lock him in the closet by accident again? She ran to the bedroom at the back of the house and opened the closet door. "Mac?" Pushing aside clothes, she rummaged around until she was sure he wasn't there.

"Come on, Mac. Where are you? Give me a clue."

A quiet meow came from the living room.

Really? He couldn't let her know he was out there when she first called? Stalking into the front room again, she looked for her trouble-maker cat. "Mac, where are you?" He wasn't in either of the stuffed chairs, nor was he on the side table where he enjoyed swatting the manger animals onto the floor.

"Mac Douglas, tell me where you are right now."

A loud meow was followed by a streak of gray fur jumping toward her. "Mac!"

Just as she caught the cat, the entire tree tilted in the opposite direction and fell against the bay window. She stared at the animal in her arms. "Now what's got into you? Since when do you climb the Christmas tree?"

The cat looked at her with its bright whiskey-colored eyes for a moment before butting his head up against her chin. She scratched between his folded ears before putting him down. "I don't know what's going on with you, but if Cam sees this tree like this, I'm not taking the blame."

Mac rubbed against her legs.

"Don't try to make up to me now. I need to get this fixed before Cam arrives." She stilled. *If* Cam arrived. He said last year it all depended on whether she started living again.

She'd tried to do just that. She'd followed-up on all the things Coco and Ian had showed her, calling Mr. Branson, introducing Luca to his two soulmates without letting him know that's who they were, accepting a few invitations to go to events with others. Now that she understood not everyone's life in town was as perfect as she'd thought, it made it a little easier to socialize.

She'd even gone back to America to visit her family and finagled a promise for her mom and John to visit her in Deervale next year. The hardest part had been being nice to the one woman in town who appeared incredibly selfish.

Sophia Dunlap had a younger sister, Thea, who had cancer and was supposed to receive a bone marrow transplant, but Sophia hadn't told a soul in Deervale that she even had a sister. Once the Spirits of Christmas Present showed her Sophia's secret dedication to her sister, Holly had found a new patience with Sophia.

It appeared she'd need new patience with her cat as well. She walked over to the fallen Christmas tree. So many of the ornaments reminded her of her time with Cam, but she'd added new ones every year because that had always been their tradition. The only ones that weren't up there were ones Mac had broken.

She scanned the room to make sure the cat wasn't causing any more trouble and found him sitting on the arm of "his" chair, cleaning his paw. Shaking her head, she grasped the tree and pulled it back upright. Luckily, it didn't go through the window. There may not be any snow on the ground, but it was cold outside, and she couldn't imagine celebrating Christmas al fresco.

The artificial tree's branches were rusty from a water leak early in the year. It was an older model where each branch needed to be inserted into its appropriate slot and the rust on the metal ends had made it a struggle to put together by herself. At least none of the branches came out when the tree tipped over. Though that may mean she wouldn't be able to take it down after the season was over.

She should have asked Brody or Ethan for help, but the tree raising and decorating had been such a personal event for her and Cam. She just couldn't do it. She should probably just buy a new tree, but she couldn't do that either. This was *their* tree.

She stepped back and viewed her masterpiece. Branches were bent and ornaments were missing. "Mac, if you broke any of my ornaments, you won't get your Christmas treat this year." She crouched down and started picking up ornaments.

Cam *had* to come. She hadn't overheard anyone calling her the "poor widow Douglas" anymore. That had to be because she was getting out and interacting with friends and neighbors. Or it could just mean she wasn't in the right places to hear it.

Mac rubbed against her knee before batting a crystal ball with a sleigh inside it completely out of her reach. "Hey, stop that. I don't remember asking you for your help." She stood and placed the ornaments on a side table then walked around to the other side of the tree.

Before searching for the ornament Mac sent rolling, and any more that had gone that way, she turned on the gas stove then hit the button that brought all the Christmas lights on, bathing the room in a pink glow. The two trains started to move, a tiny whistle signaling the start of the one beneath the tree.

Quickly, she crouched down to check the track for ornaments. Sure enough, a tiny silver bell with her and Cam's wedding date engraved on the side lay in the way of the oncoming train. Diving under the lowest branches, she snatched it up before there was a train wreck.

"I always did love your ass." Cam's voice from behind her sent her heart racing.

Scrambling from beneath the tree, she let her gaze feast on the one man that filled her heart and soul even to this day. "Cam."

"Merry Christmas Eve, hen." He floated before the fireplace in a sleeveless black t-shirt that revealed his muscled arms, his forest green, blue, and white plaid kilt which showed his bare knees, and a pair of black hiking boots. His hazel eyes were a bright green, his love for her shining in them.

Her heart burst with joy, almost taking her breath away. Swallowing against her tears of happiness, she smiled, letting him see how much she still loved him even after three years apart. "I wasn't sure you'd come."

He grinned. "It was your actions that made it possible." A brief ripple of concern crossed his brow so quickly, she wasn't sure she actually saw it.

Rising to her feet, she brushed off her green slacks. "I worked hard to be involved. I didn't want to risk never seeing you again." She stepped forward, wanting to hug him, but knew she couldn't. "Can you phase through me?"

Hurt flashed in his eyes, proving to her that his feelings hadn't changed since he'd passed, not that she'd expected any less. What must it be like on the other side?

He gave her a soft smile. "How about if I do it when I leave so I can carry your sweet scent with me?"

"You can smell me too when you do that?" She thought it was her imagination that Cam's distinctive clove-like cologne stayed with her after a "phase-through," what she'd named the experience.

He nodded. "One of the perks of phasing."

She grinned. "You mean besides flying through time?"

"Yes." He stepped closer to her.

"Will I get to do that when I cross over?" How fun would that be to fly with Cam? She wouldn't have to worry about him falling from the side of a mountain again. The thought brought a wave of anger, and she quickly squashed it.

"I hope not. I want us to enjoy eternity together, not just these few visits we've had."

"Wait a minute, do you mean after tonight I'll never see you again?" The thought brought tears to her eyes for a totally different reason than before.

Cam looked away and brushed his thick brown hair off his forehead. "I don't know yet. Each year they make it more difficult."

"They?"

His gaze snapped back to her. "I can't explain. What I do know is that a lot will have to do with the two spirits coming to visit you tonight."

She moved to Cam's old chair, the only one she was allowed since Mac commandeered hers two Christmases ago and was comfortably ensconced there, watching them. "Just tell me what you need me to do. We can do this."

Cam's face was far more serious than she'd ever seen it in life. Whatever pressures he was under were far more critical. Now that she thought about it, the wrinkles around his eyes weren't just smile lines. Wasn't death supposed to be a release?

Or is my need to see him, causing him problems?

The new thought scared her so much, she pushed it aside to think about later when he wasn't visiting. Their time together was too short as it was. "Tell me about my visitors." She forced her voice to sound upbeat.

He floated closer, perching on Mac's chair arm. "The first is Malcolm. He's a very successful spirit guide, but his methods are not the norm. If he doesn't do well on this visit, I'll be forced to let him go."

"And you don't want to do that."

He nodded. "Correct. For more than one reason, but suffice it to say his outlook on life is very pessimistic, for good reason."

"And you need me to help him see the happier side of life?" She was well aware of both sides thanks to Cam's early death, so she could certainly empathize. Still, it wouldn't be easy.

"That's part of it, but it will be made more difficult by the spirit he chose to work with."

"You let him choose? I thought you were the boss." She winked, trying to lighten the mood.

Cam shook his head. "Unfortunately, I had no say in it. I would have chosen someone else, someone less opposite of him. My fear is that Joy's unfailing optimism may make him even more resistant to change than someone who could see both sides."

Ah, now she understood. "Then it sounds like you really need me to mitigate both their views."

He smiled. "I've always loved how quick you are to catch on. Yes, but it won't be easy. These two are as far apart as Neptune and the sun."

"Maybe Malcolm chose Joy because her optimism attracts him. Maybe he secretly wishes he could be that way, too."

"I hope you're right, but I have my doubts." Cam's furrowed brow proved exactly how concerned he was. That's where his new wrinkles were.

"I'll do everything I can to make this work for them. And if Malcolm changes his ways, will I get to see you again next year?"

Cam shrugged his shoulders. "I won't know until after they leave you. I'll come back and let you know what the outcome was either way."

She was more determined than ever to make sure Malcolm kept his job because she refused to be separated from Cam until she died. That would be too hard to live with.

With determination, she rose and walked to stand in front of him, but her gaze was caught by Cam absently stroking their cat. "Now why does he get to be petted and I don't?"

He looked down at Mac, a puzzled frown on his face. "I don't know. This is the only instance I'm aware of that a phased spirit can touch something living."

She quirked her mouth up. "Well, we always knew Mac was, um…special."

Cam's laugh made her smile. She loved his laugh. It made everyone who heard it happy.

"He's not giving you any trouble, is he?"

She thought back to last Christmas Eve when Mac swiped all the manger animals onto the floor and then tonight with him climbing in the Christmas tree. She could tattle, but she didn't want to add one more thing to Cam's shoulders.

Instead, she reached down and scratched the cat behind one folded ear. "No, he's been great company. He gets feisty during Christmas, but I think he's trying to keep me occupied since you're not here to share it."

Cam rose, the space between them no more than a hand's breadth. "I so wish I was with you. I'd do anything to take back that Christmas day trip to the mountain. I thought I was invincible. How wrong I was."

She stared deeply into his eyes, the hazel mix of colors meshing into a dull gray. "I know you would, but there's nothing you can do about it now. We'll have to muddle along as best we can together. Are you okay where you are?"

He gave her a quick nod, but changed the topic. "Did you find out any more about my half-sister?"

"You knew about her and never told me?" She crossed her arms, not at all happy to find he'd hidden that fact from her their whole time together.

He shook his head. "No, I didn't know. I could never keep that from you. I learned it from Ian and Coco last year. They said you planned to try to find her."

"I did, but I only found out that the car she drove was rented in Glasgow. The car rental agency wouldn't give me any information."

"Did you ask anyone here to help you with that?"

Holy crap, she hadn't thought of that. "No. But I will. I've help now at the shop, so I have a little more time."

Cam's eyes widened before an approving smile lifted his lips. "That's very good news. I'm glad you aren't spending your life on my silly idea."

Silly idea? "Cameron Douglas, the One of a Kind Christmas Shop was not a silly idea. It was an inspired idea. People here in Deervale love it."

"I'm glad. It must be doing well, if you've hired someone on. I just don't want you to feel that you have to keep it going if it ever becomes a burden."

She walked toward their tree filled with one of kind Christmas ornaments. She wouldn't tell him that they were looking at a loss this year. Hiring Brooke had been to allow her to rejoin the community, what Cam had told her she needed to do to see him again. It had hurt the profits, but it was worth it. She turned to face him. "It could never be a burden. That shop is the closest to a child I have from you."

The brown specs in Cam's eyes seem to glow before he floated toward her. "Holly, I'm sorry I put off having a child with you. It's one of my biggest regrets. You would make an amazing mother. But don't mother the shop. It's not the legacy I want to leave you with."

Another surge of anger tried to make its way from her diaphragm to her heart, but she quickly redirected her focus. "Well, it's all I have of you now besides these visits."

He looked away as if what she said bothered him.

"Cam, is something wrong?"

"No." He didn't meet her eyes. "All I think about is you." Then as if catching himself, he looked at her. "And all my duties and the spirits under my wing. Much like you, I must move on."

She crossed her arms. "I hope that doesn't mean you forget about me in the process."

His gaze softened. "Never. You own my heart, love."

"And you own mine."

His brow furrowed.

Was he in pain? Or worried? She couldn't tell.

But then he smiled. "I have faith that you can make this visit with the spirits successful. Do your very best. You may have to change the way you think, but trust me, it will be worth it in the end."

She dropped her arms. "Well, if that isn't as clear as mud."

He laughed, the sound filling her with happiness once again.

"Are you ready for me to phase through you?"

"You have to leave already?" Her heart squeezed. Every moment with him was a joy she didn't experience the rest of the year.

"I'm afraid so, hen. My ability to stay with you even this long and not risk becoming a ghost is because I'm protected by my superior for mere minutes. But I'll be back after you finish whipping my spirits into shape."

Though he smiled, she could tell leaving her upset him as much as it upset her. It made her more confident that he'd return at the end of the night. "I'll send them back to you all fixed and ship-shape."

"I know I can count on you. Now close your eyes."

She stared at him a moment longer, memorizing his face as it was, the love in his eyes a soothing balm to her loneliness. Then she closed her eyes and waited. Two seconds later, she felt him move through her. It wasn't just his scent that filled her, but his very essence. No one could know what that was like.

The exact moment she felt him leave her body, she opened her eyes and looked up, but all she saw was his lower half floating through the ceiling. She grinned. She just loved that Scotsmen wore nothing beneath their kilts.

She looked down at Mac, who had curled up on his chair and tucked his nose beneath his tail to settle in for an evening nap. "Well, a lot of company you're going to be. Good thing I've guests arriving."

Glancing at the tree, she groaned. And a tree to fix, clothes to change into and dinner to eat before they arrived. She glanced once more at the cat before throwing her arms up and stalking back to the tree.

Chapter Three

Joy glanced at the clock in Holly Douglas' home. It was ten minutes to nine. How close did Malcolm plan to cut it? Maybe he was changing from his dark and depressing brown cloak to something more Christmassy. She hoped he could at least change the cloak's color. If he chose red, he'd look like the wolf dressed up as Little Red Riding Hood. How appropriate. Green, and he would resemble an elf, but since he was easily over six feet tall, he'd look more like Merlin.

Why did he wear a cloak? No other spirit she'd met wore a cloak. Most of them wore what they were used to wearing in life, as she did. She smoothed down her princess cut, Kelly-green velvet dress, with the wide sleeves. It brought out the green tones in her eyes and showed off her waist and calves.

The cute ankle-high matching boots had been an inspiration, not her own though. That was Mrs. Ferrisletter's suggestion, one of her old trainers from when she became a spirit guide. As usual, she'd wrapped her hair in a tight bun, a habit from her nursing days.

She looked at Holly, who had fallen asleep in her chair. Poor thing was wiped out from working at her One of a Kind Christmas Shop. The idea of every ornament and decoration being one of a kind was absolutely wonderful. Though Cameron thought of it, it was Holly that made it happen, according to the file.

Holly was dressed practically in a pair of jeans and a pretty aqua blue sweater with a white snowflake pin that had a special design in the middle, though from where Joy floated, she couldn't see what it was exactly.

She glanced at the clock again. Two minutes to nine. Where was Malcolm?

The subtle scent of bayberry caught her attention before she felt his presence behind her. She took a deep breath, nervous at how sensitive she was to him. She'd be mortified if he ever discovered she dreamed about him, never mind what those dreams were about.

Slowly, she turned to find him floating just behind her right shoulder, his face almost invisible in the darkness of his brown hood. Changing had obviously not occurred to him. "I'm glad you arrived in time. I didn't want to start without you."

He nodded but didn't say anything.

She grinned. "Don't tell me you're going to play the role of Scrooge's Spirit of Christmas Future. Don't you think that's a bit over dramatic? Not to mention far too English for a Scotsman?"

He turned toward her. "I was simply acknowledging your observation on my timeliness."

She chuckled. "Now you really sound like an Englishman."

At his scowl, she turned away, biting her cheek to keep from laughing.

The clock began to strike the ninth hour.

"Shall we?" She looked back at him. Hooking her arm within his, she pulled him forward even as his eyes widened. She was too excited to meet Holly face to face to care what he thought.

As they stopped in front of their assignment, two things struck her one after the other. The first was that the little design in Holly's snowflake pin was a fairy and beautifully etched. The second thing was that while Holly was still asleep, the large gray cat sat on its own chair staring at them.

Malcolm leaned in. "That cat shouldn't be able to see us."

She nodded, just as surprised as him.

When the grandfather clock stopped chiming, they both stared as the gray cat walked onto the arm of his chair, jumped across the short distant to the other chair where Holly slept and pounced into her lap, effectively waking her up.

"What? Really Mac?" She grabbed him up and as she lifted him onto the arm of her chair, she noticed them. "Oh, hi." Her gaze flitted to the clock before coming back to them. "Sorry. I never seem to be able to stay awake for Christmas Eve visitors. You must be Malcolm and Joy."

Joy smiled. "That's quite all right. You've had a long day, I'm sure."

"What a beautiful dress. I could never wear something like that." Holly sat straighter as she looked down. "Oh and I love your boots. I need to find a pair of those."

"Thank you." Cameron's wife was a delight. She seemed very comfortable with them.

Holly turned to Malcolm. "Malcolm, if we're going to fly away together, you must show me your face. The hood thing is all fine for drama, but we're on the same team here."

Joy pursed her lips to keep from smiling.

Malcolm acquiesced to Holly's request and dropped his hood back, revealing his scruffy chin in profile. Joy's body took notice, and she suddenly wished he'd pull it up again. The man was walking sensuality, at least to her.

"Holy crap!" Holly faced her. "Did you know he was this hot?"

Luckily, Malcolm saved her from having to answer that. "It's a pleasure to meet you, Holly. Are you ready for your journey to begin?"

Holly continued to stare at Malcolm.

Joy cleared her throat. "Holly. Holly?"

Finally, Holly turned toward her. "Yes?"

"Malcolm asked if you're ready to begin your journey?"

Holly looked back at Malcolm then returned her gaze to her. "Absolutely." She rose from the chair.

"Wonderful." Joy waited as Holly's gaze flitted back toward Malcolm before finally returning to her. She didn't really blame her. His dark good looks took some getting used to. "This visit is a little different because we're the Spirits of Christmas Future, which means that you'll see things no one else will know for years."

"And I must promise to not reveal anything I see, right?"

Malcolm nodded. "Aye. If you don't think you can keep these secrets, we'll have to skip the visit."

Holly scowled at him and crossed her arms. "Excuse me. I didn't reveal a single thing I learned from Coco and Ian's visit. I'm sure I can keep secret whatever you choose to show me."

"You must be sure."

Holly gave an exasperated sigh. "I promise."

The cat took that moment to meow loudly.

Holly turned back. "What, Mac? You have plenty of food and your litter box is clean. What else could you want? I'll only be gone minutes your time, if that."

Joy watched in fascination as the cat seemed to accept Holly's answer and proceeded to jump onto the seat of the chair Holly had just vacated and lay down.

"Really, Mac?" Holly turned to face them. "He demanded that he take my chair over there, forcing me to use Cam's. Now suddenly, he wants Cam's chair back?"

Joy shook her head. "Usually animals can't see us. He's a very special cat."

"Believe me, I know. Even Cam doesn't know why he can pet Mac."

Joy froze. That was impossible. She glanced over at Malcolm, who was looking at her as well. Somehow, she knew he agreed that something was afoot. They'd have to talk about it on their first break.

Turning back to Holly, she gave her a smile. "I understand you enjoy flying."

"I do. I mean, when I'm phased. I'm not big on airplanes. Do you want to phase me now?"

"I'd be happy too." Joy laid her hand on Holly's shoulder and phased her. The living couldn't see those who were phased. The only reason clients could see spirit guides was because Cameron made it possible before they officially visited.

Holly floated around in a circle, her smile showing exactly how much she enjoyed flying. She finally stopped in front of them. "I don't know why Cam said he hoped I wouldn't be able to fly after I die."

Again, Joy glanced at Malcolm to find him also frowning at Holly's statement. Maybe Cam hoped that Holly would serve in a different capacity after she joined him.

Now that she thought about it though, all the spirit guides were single, every one. There were definitely sexual goings-on, but no actual couples. She'd never even thought of it before. Maybe couples went somewhere else in the afterlife.

Malcolm held out his hand. "Come. It's time for your first visit."

"My pleasure." Holly slipped her hand into Malcolm's.

Joy felt a little jealousy that she was on the other side of Holly. She'd much prefer touching Malcolm, but then again, if she wanted to keep her composure, she was better off right where she was.

He looked at her as if to ask if she was ready, so she nodded, and he flew them through the high-ceiling of Holly's house on Main Street, Deervale then toward Glasgow.

Holly's smile proved her love of flying. When Erskine Cancer Center came into sight, she turned serious. "Are we going to visit Thea?"

She squeezed Holly's hand. "Yes, we are."

"I hope the bone marrow transplant went well. The poor girl spent last Christmas here."

Malcolm phased them through the roof of the building and down to the fourth floor. They stopped outside a patient room.

"Wait a minute. This is critical care."

"That's correct." Malcolm let go of Holly's hand and opened his arm toward the door.

Holly hesitated. "Is her family in there?"

Joy released her hand and patted her shoulder. "No, not yet."

Holly didn't respond. Instead, she floated through the door.

Joy turned to Malcolm. "Are you sure this is a good idea?"

He shrugged. "It's part of the reality of her future."

"I'm not so sure. It's not as if Sophia has told her about Thea. I still don't see how this will help Holly be open to change or deepen her relationships. Sophia is far too needy for Holly to take on. It just seems like additional heartache for her when she's already suffered enough."

Malcolm's eyes narrowed. "Others have suffered far worse. This is important for her to deal with and for the later ramifications."

The man's tone had lowered, almost as if he, himself, had been the one to suffer greater loss. If he planned to force Holly into feeling whatever he felt, they were not going to get along at all. "Care to enlighten me on those ramifications?"

"No." Malcolm turned away from her and floated into the patient room.

She headed for the room as well then halted. Emotional reactions to others' rudeness never worked out well. Taking a cleansing breath, she exhaled and proceeded through the wall.

Holly leaned over the sleeping eighteen-year-old. "She's so much thinner than the last time I saw her. I thought Thea was getting a bone marrow transplant."

Malcolm hovered at the foot of the bed. "She was supposed to, but they found more cancer and had to do additional chemo."

Holly's scowl was all for Malcolm, and it gave Joy a certain tiny pleasure. "And how did that go?"

"It went well." Malcolm floated to the other side of Thea's bed. "She had to gain her strength back from that and while she recuperated at home, her boyfriend kissed her, unaware that he had the flu. It compromised her immune system. They brought her here to help her, but it doesn't look good."

The tears in Holly's eyes tugged at Joy's heart, and she floated over to her, wrapping her arm around her shoulders. "I know it's hard."

Holly's head snapped around to look at her. "Are you saying she'll die?"

Joy looked away, unwilling to make the pronouncement.

Malcolm, though, had no compunction. "Aye." By the way he said it, Joy was almost sure he enjoyed telling Holly the hurtful news.

Holly narrowed her gaze at him. "When? What time period are we in. I don't see a Christmas tree in here like last year when I visited with Coco and Ian."

Malcolm's gaze didn't waver. "This is two years later and aye, it's Christmas."

Holly floated up to Malcolm. "Then how come there's no tree or decorations. Where's her family? Where's Sophia?"

Just then the door to the room opened and Sophia walked in. The smile she had on her face immediately disappeared once she saw that Thea was asleep. The woman walked past Malcolm and Holly to reach the side of the bed where Joy floated. She moved out of the way to observe Holly's reaction.

"Oh, poor Sophia." Holly pointed. "She looks haggard."

Sophia sat next to the bed and moved the blanket farther up Thea's body. "You need to pull through for me, sis. You're all I have left. Mum's and dad's house is too big for just me. I can't lose you, too."

Sophia gave a half-hearted grin. "That's right, you heard me. It's all about me. You have to live because I need you."

Joy had to steel herself against Holly's frown. She looked on the verge of tears. It would be easier to trust Malcolm if he didn't look so smug in the face of Holly's heartbreak.

Holly stared accusingly at her and then Malcolm before she fled the room.

Joy flew after her and found her down the hall in the waiting area. "I'm sorry, Holly."

"Why? Why show me this if I can't tell Sophia?"

Malcolm came up behind her. "Because it's part of your future."

Holly crossed her arms over her chest. "Really? You won't let me befriend Sophia so I can help her, and then you show me this?"

Malcolm didn't say a word and doubt crept up Joy's spine. Did he also have an alternative motive for this assignment, like Cameron? Was she the only one who simply wanted to help Holly? With anger starting to form, she shook her head. "There's no rule against you befriending Sophia."

Holly's eyes widened. "But I thought I wasn't supposed to interfere with her life. I mean, am I allowed to change the future based on what I see here?"

"Yes."

"No." Malcolm's response came at the same time as her own.

She looked at him in shock, but he was staring at Holly. "Excuse us, Holly. Obviously, we need to talk." Grabbing his hand, she whisked him back to her home. Holly would be fine as they would return at the very next second in her time.

When they arrived at her place, Joy withdrew her hand from Malcolm's and rounded on him. "What do you mean she can't change the future? That's exactly what Cameron wanted us to motivate her to do."

He solidified and strolled toward her couch. "That's not what he said. He said he wanted her to be open to change and closer relationships."

She threw her hands up, disgusted with her show of emotion, but unable to control it at the moment. "I would think instituting change is a great way of proving she's open to it, don't you think? And what could be better than forming a close friendship with Sophia?"

"Lapsir in a glass." Malcolm called for the red drink and when it appeared on her end table, he picked it up and took a sip as if he hadn't heard her.

"Malcolm. Answer me."

He lifted his gaze to hers and in a brief moment she witnessed raw pain before it was hidden behind a thoughtful countenance. "I'm simply treading carefully. Cameron is being manipulated as are we. If we don't get this right, there will be dire consequences as you already pointed out."

She solidified and rested her hands on the back of her recliner, somewhat embarrassed by her display after his calm answer. "I understand that, but even with normal cases, the whole point is to help the living see what's in store for them. It's always their decision on what to do about it. If Holly wants to befriend Sophia, then why not? Why even show her Thea if she couldn't?"

Malcolm continued to stare into the red liquor in his hand.

She took the opportunity to study him. His outside might be as hot as Holly observed, but his inside seemed a bit rough. It appeared she needed to know the inside as well if they were to get through this.

"Malcolm?"

Malcolm cursed himself for taking the shortcut through the

underground alley. What was a few more minutes delay in getting Blair home and into their bedroom? They had all night now that they were consummates.

But because he was too anxious to get her naked, they stood face to face with three criminals who didn't look like they cared one wit about life or death. He felt Blair shudder against his back. He'd die to protect her, but not until after she escaped. "What do you want?" As if he didn't know.

The smaller of the three, but the obvious leader, grinned, showing yellow teeth in a serious stage of decay. "I wouldn't mind a piece of her, but I'll settle for your bills." The man waved his gun. "But don't try anything, or we'll take her too."

He clenched his jaw to keep from vocalizing a threat that would only get them killed. "Fine." Slowly, he reached his hand down to unlatch his sporran. Pulling out his wallet, he opened it.

"Take it." The leader nodded to one of his muscle men.

The big guy grabbed at his wallet, but he pulled it back. "You said you wanted the bills."

The little guy sneered. "Just need to make sure we get *all* of them."

Schitz, this wasn't good.

The big guy pulled it out of his hand.

Stealthily, Malcolm reached behind his back to take Blair's hand and started moving away.

"Stop."

He halted as the leader trained the gun on him. He quickly put himself between his soulmate and the weapon. "What? You have what you wanted."

"What's the rush? I need to make sure it's enough."

Malcolm waited until the man's gaze moved to investigate the wallet. Then he pushed Blair behind a commercial trash receptacle.

"What the fux?" The leader looked up at him and glared. "You're a fuxing Watchman."

The two other miscreants' eyes widened before a growl issued from one and a yell from the other.

He dropped to the ground and rolled to grab up a metal pipe that had missed getting into the trash. As he rose, the first man was on him. He let the pipe precede him straight into the big man's jaw, sending him flying backwards to land flat on his back.

But the other muscle man swung, so he ducked. Unfortunately, wrestling must have been the criminal's pastime if the strength of his choke hold was any indication. As a Watchman, Malcolm had been assigned to end the underground fighting ring, which no doubt had this muscle man as a member.

But he wasn't a Watchman in just looks. Grasping the big man's arm around his throat, he bent forward, dropping to his knees, and sent the man over him, the arm loosening enough for him to twist the wrist and escape the hold. He slammed his elbow into the man's face before jumping up to defend against the kick of the first man.

He grabbed the booted foot heading for his mouth and twisted hard. The man fell to the ground moaning.

With the two biggest threats reduced, he turned to find the leader.

"Malcolm!"

Blair's scream chilled his heart. He raced toward the sound to find the leader dragging her toward the end of the alley almost to the opening to street above. If the man reached the main road, Malcolm would lose her. He raced toward them.

He *couldn't* lose her. She was his life.

His heart squeezed at the realization he wouldn't reach her in time. With nothing to lose, he yelled. "Halt or be eliminated!"

The Watchman cry had the desired effect. The leader stopped, losing his advantage.

Malcolm caught up.

The leader's furtive movements made it clear that without his muscle, he was like a cornered rat. "Stop or I'll kill her." The gun in his hand, pointed at Blair, shook.

Malcolm slowed to a stop. A hostage situation he could handle. "Let her go, and I'll let you go."

The fearful chuckle the man gave was telling. "I'm not stupid." He nodded toward the alley where the two other men still lay. "I know what a Watchman can do. I let her go and I end up with a slow death. Uh-uh, no thanks. She's my lifeline."

He'd just have to sweeten the pot. "You're smarter than I thought. I should have known the way you set up that ambush. I'll not only agree to let you go if you return her to me, but I'll never bring you in, even if I see you again. You'll look pretty impressive to your competition then."

Malcolm paused, watching the play of emotion on the man's face. He was definitely interested. "In fact, if you want to eliminate some of your competition, you can find me and give me their whereabouts. That way we both win. All you have to do is let her go."

The small man's face took on a clever gleam. "She must mean a lot to you."

Schitz. He'd made the deal too good. He shrugged his shoulders. "It's more that I'm supposed to be protecting her, and it won't look good on my record if I lose her."

"Aw, poor Watchman screwed up, out gunned by a criminal. That does sound sweet." The man's excitement at that prospect was too real.

"As good as that would feel for you, think of all the territory and followers you could gain if you take my deal."

The small man wiggled his brows. "That would be nice."

"Hand her over and it's all yours."

The man licked his lips. "It's tempting. Almost as tempting as she is." He looked at Blair, the gleam in his eye telling Malcolm a second too late that it wasn't going to work.

The gun went off and the man shoved Blair at him.

He caught her as his breath clogged in his lungs.

"Malcolm?" Her soft voice tore at his heart.

Laying her down as he sunk to the ground, he stared at the blood soaking her pretty silver dress, turning it a rusty brown. It was a fatal shot. Tearing his gaze from the sight, he looked Blair in her beautiful brown eyes. "It will be okay. We'll get you to hospital. I already hear the ambulance siren."

"I love you, Malcolm."

"I know. *Tha gaol agam ort, leannan.* Just hold on."

Her fingers found his and she squeezed. "I'll always be your sweetheart now."

He nodded, his throat too tight to say anything, but he didn't have to. Blair's eyes closed as she took her final, shuddering breath. His chest filled with pain as he lifted his face to the dark arched ceiling above and yelled out his anguish.

"Malcolm, where are you? Do you hear me?"

He didn't understand why he could hear the female voice in his head. Blair's lips didn't move. She was dead because of him.

"Malcolm." The hand on his shoulder squeezed, and he looked up to find a woman with auburn hair and exquisite upturned eyes. The scene behind her was a home with an old-fashioned Southwest American look.

He blinked. Schitz, he hadn't had that strong a memory since he first transitioned.

"Malcolm, are you all right?" Joy looked at him with honest concern.

He waved his hand. "I'm fine."

She squeezed his shoulder again. "You're not fine. You were in some kind of trance."

"It was just a memory." He shrugged to dislodge her hand, the comfort reminding him that nothing ever positive came from getting involved with a woman. *Then why did you choose her as your partner?*

He shook off his own question. Joy was the best spirit guide there was, as simple as that. Plus, he needed to prove to her the future wasn't as rosy as she hoped. Both were perfectly legitimate reasons.

She sat next to him on the couch. "Memory, my ass. You wouldn't answer me for at least twenty-minutes of living time."

He rubbed his forehead. "That wasn't just a memory then." Which meant he was being manipulated and he didn't like it. The last thing he needed was to feel that way again. Last time, he'd been manipulated, it had sent him into a tailspin that eventually ended in his own death.

Someone wanted him to remember the night Blair was killed. The question was how was he supposed to react to it. The feelings churning in his gut had nothing to do with the case, at least he hoped not.

Joy shook her head. "What was the memory? It must be important to our assignment." Her gaze held fear, not that much different from Blair's.

He stood and walked to the short, stone fireplace to look down at the cold hearth. What was he supposed to share? He didn't want to share any of it. No one in the spirit realm knew about his past while alive.

Cameron did. And probably his superiors. The more he thought about it, the more convinced he was that the higher-ups were pulling the strings, which meant he had to reveal the truth to Joy.

Every fiber of his being rebelled, but he also didn't want to lose his job. He'd never admit it to anyone, but his job made him feel like he was making a difference, even more than what he'd done after resigning his post as a Watchman.

"Malcolm, if it will make you feel better, I promise not to share anything with anyone…that is, if we succeed." Joy tucked a stray hair behind her ear, another behavior to watch on her. She may appear all together, but there were clues to the woman inside and she wasn't as sure they'd be successful as she pretended to be.

He leaned his elbow on the mantle. "The memory that flooded my mind was of the one woman I loved being shot and killed by a criminal. She died in my arms. I'm assuming I'm supposed to have some kind of emotional response to that, but it was so long ago." He couldn't quite bring himself to reveal the pain of having that old wound reopened and the self-doubt and guilt that permeated his psyche because of it.

Joy thankfully remained quiet, not offering any platitudes. He would have expected a bus load of sympathy or a polite recognition of his loss. That neither came gratified and disappointed him.

Finally, she looked at him. "No doubt the impending death of Thea sparked the memory, but I can't help but wonder at the connection to you. Could it have to do with your inability to prevent the death? Maybe it's a warning to allow Holly to interfere."

He raised his lip in disgust. "I'd agree, but the relationship is wrong. Holly doesn't even know Thea. Blair was my consummate."

The sympathy his pathetic soul needed finally showed in Joy's eyes. "Consummate? Is that a future word for wife?"

It was far more than that, but close enough. He nodded.

"I'm so sorry. That had to be devastating." Something in the tone of her voice had him studying her.

Her remarks were the very platitudes he expected. There was no deeper emotion behind them. Of course, how could there be? She didn't know him. She had no idea what he'd been through. What he'd done. How he'd died. He was like a hospice patient's family member. Someone to show sympathy toward, but not someone who meant something to her.

Her brow lowered in confusion as if she sensed his thoughts.

He looked away. "We may never know the reason for my memory, but it's another piece of evidence in this assignment."

Joy stood and walked toward him. It wasn't a saunter like Blair had, yet it was still purposeful. She took his hand in both of hers. "I'm very sorry you lost the woman you loved. I can't imagine what that must feel like."

There. There it was. The honest caring he'd hoped for…and despised. "No, you can't."

Joy flinched before she nodded and let go, turning away from him.

His gut tightened. It bothered him that he hurt her somehow, but wasn't it his goal to show her everything wasn't happy endings?

As a Watchman, he'd been given the authority to shoot if he encountered any resistance and if he killed the suspect, it was simply one extra sheet of paperwork. In the future, they didn't play around with criminals anymore, not since the bombings nine years before he died.

But with Joy, he was missing things. For every nuance he understood and cataloged, there were other actions that didn't conform to his template. *Maybe because she's not a suspect.* He ignored his inner voice. More likely it was because she was a woman. He'd proven he wasn't as good with female suspects, even after he'd gone rogue. "Let's get back to Holly. We have a lot yet to cover."

"Yes, we do." Joy took a sip of bottled water, her graceful neck attracting his gaze as she swallowed. She put the empty down on her coffee table. "But we aren't returning until we're agreed that she can change the future. I know you would have if you'd had the choice."

Aye! He would have and her words were like a kick to his gut. She was spot on. He'd go back now if he was allowed and save Blair, even if he had to die in her stead. It wasn't as if his death had amounted to anything anyway.

"Are we agreed?" At Joy's question, he returned his gaze to her. She couldn't have stood any straighter, her chin lifted slightly in her determination.

Now *that* he hadn't expected. "We're agreed." There was more to Joy than was at first obvious. She definitely had his attention.

Chapter Four

Joy held Malcolm's hand as they sped through space and time back to Holly. There had been devastating sorrow in his eyes when she'd finally gone to him, yet he'd pushed her comfort away.

She'd always thought of him as a bad boy, the type of man her mom had warned her about getting involved with, but the more time she spent with him, the more she doubted that first impression. He was mysterious because she didn't know much about him and his dark skin, swarthy looks and broad stature made her libido go into a flamenco dance. The man oozed sensuality.

To find out he'd loved a woman and lost her and barely remembered how he felt about it had made her jealous and peeved that he could be so callous. Now she knew better.

He was more like herself than she'd thought. He hid his pain and portrayed a serious, somewhat depressing and flippant attitude, while she hid behind her kindness and happy outlook. With just one real conversation with him, she already felt better about their mission.

When they floated down into the hospital to stand next to Holly, she was loath to let go of his hand, but she did. "We are agreed. You can befriend Sophia if you like and try to change her future."

Holly spun around in surprise. "Wait a minute. You two weren't gone more than thirty seconds. How could you have discussed it? Not that I'm complaining or anything."

Malcolm gave Holly a smirk. "As spirits, we can travel through time, obviously, which includes going backward to when we left you."

Holly shook her head. "I can't quite wrap my head around that, so I'll just accept your explanation." She glanced down the hall where Sophia stopped a nurse to talk in whispers. "Thank you for showing me Thea. I'm going to be a good friend to Sophia because she needs one. Maybe between the two of us, we can keep this from happening." She turned back to face them. "Will Thea survive if she gets the bone marrow transplant?"

Joy raised one shoulder. "I can't tell you. I haven't looked into her alternate futures. Malcolm said this one has the highest probability…unless your friendship changes it. I honestly can't tell you what will happen."

Holly nodded as if she understood the concept. "I can't believe any possible future could be worse than this one, so I'm going to get involved."

Malcolm touched Holly's shoulder. "You must understand that everything we show you tonight can change whether from your influence or another. We will only show you the most probable future. There may be many you want to change, but you are only one person and nothing guarantees you won't make a situation worse."

"I understand." Holly looked to her. "Where to next? This place is getting a bit depressing."

Joy smothered a triumphant smile that Holly would ask her for a happier environment. "I agree. Let's look in on some people you have helped and see what they're up to tonight."

Holly held out her hand and she grasped it. Looking at Malcolm, who appeared to be staring off into space again, she forced a smile, hoping he wasn't in another trance already. "Malcolm, will you be joining us?"

He redirected his gaze to her and nodded. As soon as he took Holly's hand, Joy flew them through the roof of the hospital toward Deervale.

As they drew closer, a long line of cars could be seen on Main Street, the red brake lights adding color to the newly fallen snow.

"Well, what's going on down there? Is the light in front of the church broken?"

Joy grinned and kept them hovering above the two-lane road. On one side was a long white-washed building connected to a row of stone buildings, typical in Deervale. Across the street was the Parish Church which made the snow even more colorful with its lit stained-glass windows.

The double doors of the church were thrown wide as people filed in by the pairs and in groups, all chatting and obviously in a good mood. "I believe the cause of this minor traffic congestion is the church, not the light."

Holly pulled her hands from both of them and floated closer to the building. "Is it midnight? Maybe midnight services on Christmas Eve."

Joy laughed. She loved happy occasions. "Oh, this has nothing to do with Christmas. Not really. It's only half past seven as they say in this town."

Holly looked back at her in confusion. "Are you going to tell me, or let me figure it out for myself?"

Malcolm answered for her. "You'll figure it out."

Joy touched his shoulder. "If you don't want to watch this, I understand."

"Why? Our ceremonies in the future are a lot less involved. It's not like I've something else I need to do." The irritation in his tone told her a lot more about how he felt than his words.

Maybe this would be helpful for him to see. They floated closer to the doors of the church where Holly was.

"Look at everyone. I think the whole town is here and then some." Holly pointed to the long line of people walking quickly toward the steps.

"You're probably right." Joy grinned. "And if I'm not mistaken, you've already arrived."

"Me? Now this will be interesting. How many years in the future are we?"

Malcolm frowned. "Only four."

Joy rolled her eyes at Holly. "He doesn't consider this the future compared to his time period."

"Well, Malcolm, exactly how many years ahead of us are you, anyw—Oh, look." Holly pointed behind them.

Joy turned around. It appeared Milly Bryden was getting married in style.

"It's farmer Campbell's sleigh! It's beautiful!" Holly floated out to the street as the brown sleigh covered in white bunting was pulled into the church drive by two matched draft horses.

Malcolm leaned into her. "Good thing they didn't clear the streets well or those blades would be ruined."

Joy snapped her head around. "Try not to be a scrooge."

He raised both his eyebrows in surprise. "I'm not a scrooge."

"Then enjoy the happiness here. Let it fill your heart and seep into your bones." At his perplexed expression, she turned back to watch Holly. Had the man forgotten how to be happy? Her irritation dissolved at that sad thought.

"It's Milly!" Holly floated back to them as the old farmer pulled the sleigh to a stop in front of the church doors.

The few people left milling about there immediately approached the sleigh. Milly's father stepped down first then helped his daughter out.

Holly's smile was wider than the street. "She's so lovely. I've never seen her hair down. She always wears it up, like you. I can't do that. Mine is too thick. It gives me a headache." Holly looked back at her for a moment. "Is your hair thick?"

She shook her head, and Holly was back to watching the scene.

The scent of bayberry alerted her to Malcolm leaning in again. He whispered in her ear. "Dinna ye let yers down on occasion?"

She was sure the delightful shiver that raced across her skin was noticeable to him, but she refused to turn her head. "No, I don't. Since when do you have a Scottish accent?"

"We all have the brogue, lass. We just decide when ta use it."

She gave him a scowl. "You don't need to be using it on me. We need to concentrate on our mission."

His lips quirked up. "I dinna ken I disturbed yer concentratin'."

She wanted to throw her hands up and stalk away, but Holly was nearby. Instead, she settled for ignoring him and drifting toward Holly.

Maybe the happiness of the occasion was starting to seep in with Malcolm, but if his Scottish accent was a result of that, she'd rather he remained dour. It was bad enough she was interested in him and dreamed about sex with him. She didn't need to have him using that accent on her.

"Tell me she's marrying Luca." Holly's hopeful expression was too hard to resist.

"Yes, she is, thanks to you introducing them."

"Now, that was only because Coco told me they were soulmates." Holly gazed past her and squinted at Malcolm, who had floated over. "And I never told them I knew that. All I did was make sure they met." Holly crossed her arms to punctuate her statement.

"I'm glad to hear it."

Joy ignored him. "I had no doubts."

"Can we go inside now?" Holly drifted toward the church. "I'd love to see her walk down the aisle. Did Luca ever stop growing? He made me feel like an elf when he came into the store to buy Milly an ornament the other day."

Joy didn't answer immediately. It wasn't time for Holly to see herself yet. She wasn't ready for her own future.

"You've already seen the bride. Do you have to see the groom?" Malcolm's negative attitude was back to dour.

She should be careful what she wished for. "I think we can hang in the back and watch the bride meet the groom. After all, we have plenty of time." She looked at Malcolm. "Besides, what's better than a wedding?"

At the look of sorrow on his face at her words, she wished she could take them back. She softened her tone. "If you want to wait for us out here, that's fine. I realize this isn't a man's favorite event."

He just shrugged and followed Holly inside.

Men could be so stubborn. She sincerely hoped he wasn't hurt by watching. Knowing he'd lost the woman he loved gave her so much sympathy for him that she was now worried. It was much easier thinking he'd never settled on one woman.

She finally followed, floating into the church, not unaware of the irony that she'd never found *the one* herself...though she'd thought she did.

Malcolm made sure Holly stayed where she couldn't see herself. If she did, it could jeopardize everything.

Joy's attitude was already causing him serious irritation. Now that she knew about Blair, she kept looking at him like he might break. He needed to find out what was beneath her caring exterior.

His brogue had definitely affected her, but in a completely different way. Still, he'd seen a crack in her composure similar to her anger at her home. He hadn't used his brogue or had sex since he'd transitioned to the afterlife, but if it helped him figure her out then it might be worth the risk.

The rules were different now. He didn't have to worry about someone killing the woman he loved, but this assignment could very well be a set-up.

Just like Coira—his wife.

He rarely thought about the woman he'd married years after Blair's death. He'd done it out of pity, saving someone from the hellish underground, who thanked him by betraying him to a crime chief. Coira wasn't worth his time. She only served to remind him how stupid he'd been.

No, having sex with Joy wasn't a good idea. He needed to get inside her head another way. Not just because he wanted her to come out of this assignment with a new appreciation for the future, but because he needed to know how much he could rely on her...if at all.

He sensed her presence even before her minty scent filled his nostrils. The bride was about to start up the aisle, the music announcing her as everyone stood.

Holly floated higher.

He grabbed her hand, forcing her down. "You can watch from here only."

She rolled her eyes at him, but remained where he put her.

Floating back to where Joy hovered, he clasped her hand. At her startled expression, he pulled her out of the church and through the ether.

"Where are we going?"

He didn't answer since the ether parted, and she could see the green mountains of northern Argyll. Flying them down between two one-thousand-footers, he pulled her through the roof of his cottage. Once inside, he let her go and solidified.

She solidified as well and viewed his living area.

He made himself comfortable in his Barra Chair, the seat and back conforming to his body as he settled in.

Joy didn't say a word. She wandered around the room, studying everything, the blank white-washed walls, the log beams holding the thatched roof, even the plain brown couch. She paused next to an antique side table beneath a shuttered window. If she expected to see pictures of Blair or Coira, she'd be disappointed. They belonged to his former life and had no bearing on this one. *Sure, they didn't.*

She finally faced him. "Is this a replica of where you lived in Scotland?"

"Aye. The last place I lived. I moved here from Glasgow."

"It doesn't look very futuristic. In fact, it seems like something from the past."

He understood her confusion since the futuristic pieces, at least to her time frame, were not obvious. "I'm not a century ahead of you. Probably about fifty years or so, but I bought this as a holiday home when I wanted a break from the city. I moved into it permanently in the end."

She meandered to the only other chair in the room and perched on the edge of it. When she suddenly stood and looked back at it, he couldn't contain his laughter.

"The Barra Chair is from my time period. It will adjust to your shape." He held his hand out. "Go ahead."

Joy glanced down at the chair before carefully sitting in it. "Wow, I can see how this would be of great help to people with back pain."

He clamped his jaw tight to keep from responding with a sarcastic comment about her no longer being a nurse. That wouldn't help him figure her out.

"Your place is rather…sparse."

He crossed his legs at the ankle, his chair shifting with him. "I like it that way. My life became too complicated in Glasgow. I like the simplicity of this area, the standing stones, and the scenery. Open the shutters."

The dark wooden shutters snapped back against the walls, flooding the room with an opaque light that had just a hint of green in it, the ever-present mist reflecting off the grass on the surrounding mountains.

Joy smiled in appreciation. "It's beautiful. I bet it's spectacular when there's no fog."

He refrained from telling her there were no clear skies here. He didn't bring her here to talk about the weather. "Why did you want Holly to see Luca marry Milly?"

The change in subject caught her attention. She folded her hands in her lap and crossed her legs, bringing his attention to her thighs where the green velvet lay. He couldn't tell which would be softer to the touch.

She shrugged. "After the visit to Thea, I thought that one appropriate. I wanted her to see that some of her efforts over the year did bear fruit."

"But that isn't our charge. Are you saying that the visit to the church would in no way help her open herself to new experience?"

"Of course not." She moved her gaze to the window view. Her head cocked slightly to the right. "I want her to be open to the possibility of love, to see what could be in store for her as well."

If she hadn't moved her head, he would have believed her, but his training as a Glasgow Watchman kicked in. "You didn't mention that while we were there."

She moved her gaze back to him. "It wasn't time. I plan on doing it later, when she's ready."

He didn't shake his head, forcing himself to hold her gaze. She wasn't that hard to read...to him. "You brought her there so *you* could go."

"What?" She broke eye contact, even as she waved his comment aside. "Why would I want to go? Except, perhaps, to cheer up after that harsh visit to the hospital."

He rose from his chair, positive he'd found a vein. His height, already an advantage in their solid forms, would be more so now with her sitting. He took the two steps to bring him directly in front of her, forcing her to look up. "You wanted to attend the wedding of the soulmates. Why?"

She frowned. "I told you why."

"No, you told me why you brought Holly there, but that wasn't the main reason we made that visit."

A flash of pain in her blue eyes reflected her thoughts before she scowled at him. "I don't know what you're trying to intimate, but you're way off track." She uncrossed her legs and stood, about to walk by him.

He grabbed her by the shoulders. "Tell me."

Her eyes widened before she looked down and tried to twist away. "What are you doing? We're supposed to be helping Holly. Why are you attacking me?"

He didn't let go. There was too much at stake, but he was careful not to hurt her. "Joy, we have to be honest with each other. There's more going on here than simply Holly's need to be ready for her own life without Cameron."

She scowled up at him. "You keep saying that, but what evidence do we really have?"

His lips quirked up of their own accord. "How about the fact I had a trance induced memory of something I haven't thought of since I transitioned? How about the fact that I was told if I'm not successful doing it 'their' way instead of mine then this will be my last assignment?"

She stilled. "They told you that?"

He nodded.

"So, when you said if you were a failure, Cameron would

be too, you meant you would no longer be a spirit guide if you failed?"

"Correct."

"And if Cameron is a failure then that means a terrible future for Holly."

He wouldn't say that, but if she thought that, she might open up and hopefully give him an idea of what was really going on with their assignment. Seeing her vacillate, he nudged, "Tell me why you chose Luca and Milly's wedding…please."

Her gaze flitted away before she would meet his eyes again. Her slender throat revealed her hard swallow before she spoke. "I wanted to witness a marriage that would last forever."

"Why?" He kept his voice low, as if he sympathized with her. That was what he'd been taught.

"I was in love once, too."

That was different from what she'd said earlier, that she didn't have time to find a husband. Then again, she cocked her head slightly to the side at the time. "What happened?"

She twisted beneath his hands, and he let her go, giving her room to choose her words, her story. He'd decipher what he needed to once she started to talk.

Joy moved around behind the chair she'd been sitting in and grasped the back of it. That was a position she'd taken at her own home. A defense mechanism? With him? Or everyone?

"Alan was a good man. We'd been seeing each other for well over a year. I could tell he was thinking of proposing and I was ecstatic." Her smile didn't quite reach her eyes. Not surprising.

He didn't say anything, letting her decide when to continue. It was more likely to be closer to the truth than if he pushed. He hadn't had many suspects with her personality, but enough to know she would tell the truth if he let her.

She looked down at the chair as if viewing her life on the

seat. "He'd talked often about having a family, getting a place up in Prescott where we all could go during the hottest months in the valley." She glanced at him. "That's what we call the greater Phoenix metropolitan area."

He nodded to show he understood, his patience waning, but his training kept him quiet.

"I thought the idea was lovely, but never explained to him why it might not work like that for us." She paused again.

Did she let her career get in the way of her happiness? In a way, it was ironic when compared to how his career had ruined his.

Joy gripped the top of the chair so hard, he noticed it adjust away from her pressure.

"I tried to tell him as soon as I realized his intentions, but it never seemed the right time and the couple times I started to, we were either interrupted or I lost my nerve. He was such a good man. Finally, the day came that I both wanted and dreaded. He proposed."

And what did you say? The thought begged to be spoken, but at the same time he noticed his hands had curled into fists. He forcibly relaxed. Rule number one, never get involved with a suspect. If he did that, he'd lose all his objectivity. *But she's not a suspect. She's your partner.*

Joy was back to staring at the chair seat. "I said yes, of course. I loved him with all my heart. But before he could slide the beautiful diamond solitaire onto my finger, I curled my hand and told him the truth."

Her gaze finally lifted to meet his. "I told him I couldn't have children. I told him of the genetically malfunctioning uterus I once had and how the doctors said it had to be removed when I was sixteen. I assured him I was happy to adopt as I always saw myself as a mother and even grandmother."

Despite his trained objectivity, Malcolm's gut spasmed with

anger. The pain in Joy's watering eyes told him the end of her story, and he wanted to bash the man that had hurt her so much.

Oblivious to his feelings, she continued with her tale. "He closed the lid on the ring box and rose. He was shocked. He wanted to know why I hadn't told him before? Why I had let him fall in love with me when I couldn't give him the family he wanted. I tried to tell him we still could have a family. There were so many ways to do that, but he just kept shaking his head. He was actually in tears." Her own tears cascaded down her cheeks, and she wiped them away carefully with her index finger, obviously concerned about her make-up.

It took all his willpower to remain standing on the other side of the chair she used as a shield. He wanted to take her in his arms and tell her the man didn't deserve her.

Why?

Only because she was his partner. That was it. He just wanted to offer her comfort because he couldn't have her an emotional mess. That's the only reason he had to clasp his hands behind his back to keep from going to her.

She gave a half-hearted chuckle and attempted a smile. "After that, I refused every wedding invitation I received, and there were many. I know it was silly, but I just couldn't stomach seeing people so happy when my love affair ended so terribly. I was on a wedding strike."

Now the trip with Holly made sense. She'd called off her strike. "But why Luca's wedding in particular?"

This time her smile was real. "Because Coco was right. They *are* soulmates. Their marriage lasts forever."

"The happily ever after you never got."

She nodded then shrugged. "Silly, I know, but I really do think that the wedding can come in handy later. Don't you?"

He didn't disagree. He held out his hand. "Come here."

She strolled around the chair and stood to the side of him,

though she didn't take his hand. Not that he could blame her. He now knew she had some depth, which made him trust her abilities enough to work with her.

He motioned toward the chair. "Please."

She gave him a regal nod and took her seat again.

He didn't resume his. Instead, he walked to the window and put his back to it, well aware it would leave his face in shadow. "All three of us, you, myself, and Holly, have suffered the loss of a loved one in three different ways."

"Of course! You're right. So how does that fit into the larger scheme of things? Neither you nor I had a second chance."

His wife popped into his mind, but he brushed that away. They were never consummates, so her influence on him was minimal. "But Holly could have." *And so could they.*

Where the fux had that come from? Unless they had a chance to reunite with the ones they loved. The thought wasn't as comforting as it should be, probably because he was wrong.

Joy frowned. "Yes, she could, but I'm not sure how we can possibly make that happen. She is completely in love with Cameron."

"The file said Holly had two soulmates. Cameron was one, but Ethan was the other. She's already aware that a person can have more than one since she said Luca has two. My question is, when Cameron said he wanted her to be open to new experiences and deeper relationships, do you think he intends for her to be willing to love again?"

"Oh, I can't see Cameron being happy with that." Joy shook her head.

"But Cameron isn't calling the shots here." And if that was the case and he did get Holly to see she could love again, would he be allowed to keep his job, only to have his boss hate him? Was he in a no-win situation?

Joy tucked a stray strand of hair behind her ear. "I'm not liking this at all. Maybe he meant for her to find a new passion in life, like a new job or project."

"Do you really think that's the case?" He waited for her to come to the same conclusion that he had. It didn't take long.

Her shoulders slumped. "No, I don't, but there's a chance." She rose from the chair again and strolled toward him. "I want to check on something before we take Holly to her next visit." Joy actually shivered before continuing. "I'll meet you back at the church."

He studied her, but saw no hidden agenda in her movements or eye contact. "Fine, but we won't stay long there. Holly isn't going to want to stay if she can't move closer and we can't let her see herself there."

Joy nodded. "I know." She paused before she continued. "Thank you for not laughing at my stupid love story. My only excuse is I wasn't thinking with my brain."

Schitz, he would never laugh at her. "No, you were thinking with your heart."

"You're a good man." She touched his arm then rose up on her toes and kissed him on the cheek.

The contact was electrifying, literally. He jumped back as she did.

She had her hand to her lips.

"What the fux was that?" He rubbed his cheek. "Are you okay?"

She ran her finger along her lips, an erotic gesture under any circumstances. He squelched his runaway thought.

"Yes, I'm okay. That wasn't just static electricity, was it?" She looked down as if to check to make sure there was no possibility that a rug had caused the shock.

"No, it wasn't." It was more like opposites repelling.

"Maybe it's in your house. You might want to look into that."

"Right." That wasn't all he was going to look into.

"I'll see you at the church."

He nodded as she phased. Ever the lady, she floated across the room away from him before rising up through the ceiling, denying him a look beneath her dress.

He grinned. If he wanted to, he could get a glimpse of her sweet ass as easily as he'd glimpsed beneath her façade, but that wasn't his way. If he decided he wanted sex with her, she would know it up front. And if that moment ever happened, he hoped she said no…for both their sakes.

Chapter Five

Joy took a couple deep breaths, still a bit rattled from the shock. That had been too unnerving, in more ways than one. They had flown in holding hands and she'd touched him on the arm before kissing his cheek, so why the shock?

Feeling a bit more composed, she knocked on Cameron's door. "Come in."

One more deep breath and she entered. "Hi, Cameron."

"Joy, what a surprise." He smiled as he stood and came around his desk to welcome her.

She smiled politely as she slid into the chair he'd pulled over for her, happy to sit.

Cameron leaned against his desk and looked at her. "How's it going?"

"It's going well, I think."

"Is my wife happy?"

At his odd question, she took a closer look at her supervisor. His hair was messed and it looked like he hadn't slept. That never happened in the spirit realm. "Yes, she's happy. She loves flying and we just brought her to Luca and Milly's wedding."

"What?" The concern in his face had her answering quickly.

"Don't worry. We haven't let her see herself. We don't want to influence the outcome."

Cameron nodded. "I should have known. You're one of my best guides." The concerned gaze he gave her made her nervous.

"I think Holly is already open to some change. She's interested in befriending Sophia."

"Sophia?" Cameron's eyes widened. "Ach, I didn't see that coming. That is definitely a baby step in a new direction."

Baby step? "Cameron, what would you consider a giant leap? It would help if we had a bit more clarification on your expectations."

"I…I can't be more clear than that. I'm sorry."

"Is it true if we aren't successful, Malcolm will lose his job?"

Her supervisor moved his hair off his forehead. "Yes."

"Does that mean he'll be disintegrated?"

"What?" He moved away from his desk, turning as he strode back around. "I don't know where you came up with that idea."

"From Coco and the file."

He shook his head but didn't look at her. "He's not giving you any trouble, is he? I know his methods are not the norm. Is he changing at all?" The note of hope in Cameron's voice was obvious.

She answered carefully. The one thing she'd learned from her life was never to play with someone's hope. "I think a little, but I can't be sure. I don't know what he was like before. I only saw him once in a while, and we didn't have any long conversations."

"And now? Are you having lengthy conversations?"

She could smile at that. "Yes, we are."

"Good. Good."

"Cameron, why did you assign me to this case? You knew our outlooks were totally different."

He sighed. "I didn't choose you. I let Malcolm choose who he wanted to help him. He chose you."

"He did?"

Cameron nodded.

Malcolm chose her? Why? A seed of hope blossomed in her heart. Did he like her? Maybe he wanted to change but couldn't without her help. Could it be that simple?

Her supervisor pushed his hair off his forehead once again, his brow wrinkled with worry. "I'm sorry you had to be involved with this assignment. It can't be easy working with Malcolm, and this is a very difficult task."

"It helps to know he asked for me in particular." She smiled. "That must mean he actually wants my help."

Cameron's brow didn't change. "I doubt that. Malcolm doesn't accept help from anyone, least of all from women."

Her hope shriveled up and died as nothing more than a bud. "Why?"

He opened his mouth then shook his head. "I'm sorry, I can't tell you that. Ask Malcolm."

Ask Malcolm why he wouldn't accept help from women? She had a very strong feeling he'd refuse to answer. Then again, if he did, it might mean that he'd started to trust her. He *did* tell her about Blair. "Does it have anything to do with his death?"

At Cameron's surprised look, she had her answer, but he didn't elaborate. "Like I said, you need to ask Malcolm."

She rose from her seat. "Is there anything else you can tell me that might help us be successful with Holly?"

Cameron frowned, his middle finger tapping a steady beat on the desk as he thought.

She almost thought he wouldn't answer, but then he grinned as if he'd found a loophole.

"Yes. Don't be subtle."

"Don't be subtle?" She frowned at him. She'd expected a revelation about Holly or someone in their lives.

Cameron. "Don't be subtle."

She gave him a frown and turned away. She'd hoped to clarify a few things, but she'd become more confused.

"Joy?"

She had on her hand on the doorknob, but twisted around to look at him. "Yes?"

"Please help my wife." Cameron's gaze was anguished.

She sucked in her breath at his look. "I will. I promise."

She turned back and exited the office. Once outside, she paused. She *had* to help Cameron and Holly. They were suffering so much. And she had to help Malcolm.

Surprised at Cameron's unwillingness to share Malcolm's death with her, she held out her hand. "Malcolm MacLachlan's life file." She waited, but no file appeared. Since files could be read or shown like a movie, she rephrased her request. "Show me Malcolm MacLachlan's life file."

Still, nothing happened. "Show me Malcolm MacLachlan's death." Again, nothing changed. Now that was odd. Was his file locked? Did Cameron do that or as Malcolm said, were they being manipulated by some entity above Cameron.

For the first time, she felt serious concern for herself. Entities above Cameron were extremely powerful as she'd been taught in her Spirit Guide training. Yet all she had to go on was to not be subtle. So, they needed to be blunt with Holly?

Malcolm certainly hadn't been subtle when he pried into her love life. Why had he done that? Was he concerned about her as a person. He *did* choose her to work with. Or was he simply figuring out what made her tick so he could determine how much he could depend upon her.

It irked a little in hindsight. She'd never let her personal life dictate her work life. Not even while she lived. *But you did go to Luca's wedding.* She swallowed at the nudge from her conscience. It would all come full circle with Holly…hopefully.

If she was caught up in the plans Cameron's superiors had for

Holly and even Malcolm, then the weight of her responsibility to help just doubled.

Which begged the question, who would help her?

~~*~~

Malcolm stared at the paper in Holly's file. It wasn't what was written, but what wasn't. Nowhere did it say that Holly should fall in love again, but that was obviously what needed to happen. He'd dismissed the whole "soulmate" idea when he'd first read it, but after recognizing the similarity in his, Joy's and Holly's lives when it came to love, he was positive that's what the higher-ups were looking for.

He wasn't as sure that was what Cameron wanted from their visit. If he had, he would have said so. Unless he wasn't allowed to.

Malcolm dropped the file on Joy's coffee table where she'd left it. It was probably safer here than at his cottage. He scanned the room. Her place was like her, neat with everything in its proper place. At least that's how it appeared.

Walking to the double doors off the living room, he opened them. Ah, her bedroom. Here is where her secrets would be. He strode directly to her dresser. Opening the jewelry box, he sifted through the southwestern pieces, looking for a false bottom. There was nothing there. "Return the jewelry to the way it was before I opened the box." Immediately, everything shifted back.

He opened her drawers and looked beneath camisoles and underwear, yoga pants and sports bras, even a few sweaters and a pair of jeans. Nothing hidden. Moving toward the bed, he grinned.

The padded headboard would be a plus if sex got too rough. He very much doubted that ever happened with Joy. He could see her enjoying missionary style sex, or perhaps riding a man because that way her hair wouldn't get too mussed in that bun of hers. Despite his harsh thoughts, his balls tightened at the image of Joy naked and rocking on her idiot boyfriend.

The headboard was more likely a fashion statement. Joy was very concerned with how she appeared to others, not just in looks but in actions. It was less an ego thing and more a need to be liked and helpful. He'd found he was most helpful when he didn't appear kind.

Bending, he opened the single drawer in the nightstand. Heat raced to his groin. Inside, in neat rows, was at least a dozen sex toys. From various sized vibrators, to butt plugs to a double dildo with one thick side for the vagina and a thinner side for the ass. His cock, which hadn't had attention from the opposite sex since he'd transitioned, came to life in an instant. His balls tightened and need overtook him.

Slamming the drawer shut, he spun away, stalking to the other side of the bed. Nothing could surprise him now about his supposedly prissy partner. He stood in front of the second nightstand taking deep breaths, allowing his cock to return to a more comfortable state.

Once he was thinking better with his larger head, he opened the draw, secretly expecting to find a gun. He stared in shock. His own face stared back at him in a small frame. He'd never seen the photo before. He was in his hooded cape but had no shirt on, and it looked as if he was in the process of pulling the hood up. Behind him were the mountains that surrounded his cottage.

A tiny chain was hooked to the corner of the frame, but the other end was beneath the picture. He lifted it out and froze as the end of the chain settled in his palm. His whole body felt as if it would combust and his cock pushed hard against his kilt.

Joy had a piercing? It was the only explanation for the small barbell piece of jewelry in his hand. There were only three hidden places he'd seen women wear those—the belly button, the nipple and the clit. That it dangled from a dainty chain attached to a picture of himself caused more physical and emotional reactions than he could count.

He sat on the bed, staring at the small gold jewelry. The prim and proper nurse from Scottsdale had a very kinky side and obviously indulged. His palms began to sweat as he thought of touching those long legs of hers, running his hands up her inner thighs until his fingers found her moist folds, while his mouth caught one of her nipples only to discover the barbell?

He swallowed hard at the thought of using his tongue to flick it.

What did his picture mean? Did she have it because she'd planned all along to invite him to her bedroom? Or was it her way of getting turned-on? Both ideas upended his conclusions about Joy.

Joy. Did she find joy in sex? More than even he did?

He threw the picture back in the drawer and closed it. He wasn't here to pry into Joy's personal sex fetishes. He was here to figure out what Cameron's supervisors were doing. His gaze snapped back to the drawer. They could very well have planted those items for him to find, throwing him off his stride.

Nothing could be trusted. No one could be trusted. Pulling his hood over his head, he phased quickly and flew into the ether. Until he could determine if Joy's sex life had anything to do with their assignment, he would continue on his planned path. One way or another, he would discover the real reason Cameron was forced to put him on this assignment.

He landed beside Holly in the church, arriving a second before Joy did.

She gave him a kind smile. "I discovered something."

Holly turned at Joy's voice. "You did?"

"Yes, but now we need to leave here and check in on another friend of yours."

Holly looked back toward the aisle. Milly had reached the end and her father handed her over to Luca. "We can't watch the rest of the wedding?"

Joy shook her head. "I'm afraid not. You have a lot to see tonight. Besides, you don't want to spoil it by seeing it before you attend in real time, do you?"

Holly glanced at the bridal couple one more time. "I guess not."

Malcolm barely heard the conversation, his concentration on Joy's breasts. Is that where the barbell was as he'd envisioned? Could he tell through the green velvet dress, or was the thicker material, bra and camisole beneath all part of her way of hiding it?

"Malcolm?"

He raised his gaze to her face. "Aye?"

"I asked if you wanted to lead the way."

Fux, he'd already lost his focus. "Aye, take my hands."

Joy glanced at him in surprise, but she took his hand and Holly took the other.

He was glad no shock came from their clasped hands. Did their last shock run through her body and the metal jewelry she wore?

She squeezed his hand, and he quickly flew them up and westward.

He moved his focus from Joy to Holly. Holly was their assignment and she was the one he should concentrate on. At the moment she smiled, her love of flying an interesting trait. Many of the living he'd helped weren't excited about it. They said they felt as if they would fall, but since they would float in one place if he let go of their hand, it didn't make sense to him.

He could better understand those with an irrational fear of heights. That wouldn't go away just because a person was made weightless. That was exactly why it was an *irrational* fear. But Holly obviously loved it as she'd said.

"Where are we headed?" Holly looked at him, anticipation shining in her brown eyes.

Showing her the wedding had been a mistake. He should have

never agreed to it. Now she would expect her future to be rosy and that was hardly the case. "We're headed to America."

"Oh, to see my family? I just saw them at the beginning of the year, as I promised. Everyone was doing well, though it was hard to resist the pressure they put on me to move back."

He pounced on that. "Why didn't you?"

"I can't. Being in Deervale makes me feel closer to Cam."

He barely refrained from rolling his eyes. Getting her to think of others in more than a superficial way would prove tough. "But you have no family in Scotland. All the people that love you are in America. It must be hard for them to have you so far away."

Holly's brows knit together. "I suppose, but they have each other."

"And so could you."

Joy squeezed his hand, and he glanced her way to find her scowling at him once again. He ignored her look and flew them through the ether to a few years ahead. When they emerged from it, they were flying over Holly's home state of New Hampshire.

"Look at all the trees!" Joy's eyes were wide.

Holly spoke across him. "Haven't you ever been to New Hampshire?"

Joy shook her head. "I was born and raised in the Southwest and none of my living clients lived here. Are there many people? It's hard to see houses."

Holly chuckled. "Oh, there are, and even a few small cities, but my mom and John live in the northwest area and there are a lot of trees."

He'd forgotten what it was like to gaze at something in awe. His years as a Watchman had inured him to surprise and wonder.

"It's so…green." Joy was right.

In the middle of this summer day, with the sun shining brightly, the area *was* green, dark green like parts of the highlands where the reforestation tracks of evergreen trees were plentiful. Not like the mountains where his cottage sat which were a lighter green made of grass and mosses.

"Oh, there's the grocery store my mom goes to." Holly pointed with her free hand. "And that's the park where they set off the July fourth fireworks."

"It's a beautiful town, Holly." Joy's gaze moved over the landscape. "I even see some lakes here."

Holly nodded as he began to descend. "The biggest one in this area is where mom and John live. I grew up with the lake as my backyard."

He addressed Holly. "It sounds like you have a lot of memories here, too, yet you remain in Deervale."

Holly lost her smile, and his hand received a squeeze from Joy, which he ignored once again.

He brought them down through the roof of the local bank, the old farmhouse having been remodeled to better house the commercial enterprise, complete with a modern addition in the back that couldn't be seen from the road.

Holly winked at him. "I thought spirits didn't need money."

He hovered high in a corner of the main lobby where they could see behind the tellers, down the hall and the front doors. Then he released their hands.

There were a couple people at the teller stations and a financial representative headed out back. The front doors opened and two men strode in.

"It's John and Uncle Jerry. He's not really my uncle, but he and John have been best friends since high school." Holly floated out toward the center of the main area. "I call John 'dad' even though he didn't come into our lives until I was a teen. That was after the fire when the Tinders took us in. Are they still alive?"

Holly's worry over the elderly couple who were John's parents was good to see, but she had no plans to visit them and they were feeling their age. He wanted to ask her why she cared, but Joy answered instead.

"They are, but they are having health issues like most people their age."

"Maybe I should plan another visit."

"Maybe you should." He gave her a stern look. "Or you could move back here."

Holly squinted her eyes at him before floating away toward her adopted parent.

Joy started to drift after Holly, but he grabbed her arm. "Wait." He held her until Holly had moved to the other end of the lobby. Pulling Joy back to him, he kept his voice low. "You said at the church that you discovered something new. What is it?"

Her slight smile faded and worry creased her brow. "Cameron wants to tell us more, help us, but you're right, his hands are tied by others. However, after thinking very hard, he gave me a hint."

He waited patiently for her to go on, his gaze wandering from her eyes to her lips.

"He said, 'don't be subtle.'"

That caught his attention. "Don't be subtle?"

"Yes. I wasn't sure what he meant at first, but when I thought about what we want Holly to learn from her visits, it started to make sense."

"That's probably the most help we're going to receive on this assignment. We need to use it to its maximum. Good work."

Joy's cheeks turned a rosy hue at his compliment. It immediately reminded him of the photo of himself in her nightstand drawer. Was he more than a sexual fantasy for her? Even that was still a piece of information he was attempting to fit into the profile of Joy.

He pushed away the Joy project for the one they were working on together. If they weren't supposed to be subtle then his methods would work better than Joy's, so where did that leave him if the only way for him to keep his job was to change his methods?

He curled his hands into fists, beyond frustrated.

"Malcolm?" Joy was looking at him with that worried expression again.

He hated that. "Let's see how she reacts to this incident." He waved his hand toward the bank scene before them.

She drifted closer and lifted his hood from his head. "You look friendlier without that. I think this look works better with Holly." She blushed again, making him conclude that maybe it was actually Joy who liked him better without the hood.

She floated away, her slender waist catching his eye. Maybe it was her belly button that was pierced.

He shook his head to get the thought out of his mind. For all he knew, she had no piercing at all. Maybe it was just a symbol of what she thought *he* liked. If so, she was a good guesser, because the possibility that she had a piercing had his body interfering with his thought process.

Forcing himself to concentrate on the problem at hand, he followed Joy to the other side of the bank lobby where Holly hovered.

Holly watched as John went into the back with a bank employee and Jerry waited in line for a teller. "I wonder why John is here. I can't imagine him getting a loan. He's really good with money." Holly floated over to them to peek down the hall. "Maybe he needs something from his safe deposit box."

Joy threw him a worried look.

The bank doors opened. "Everybody get down on the ground, on your stomachs and no one will get hurt." A gunman with a ski mask waved a semi-automatic while another man ran for the teller counter. The customers obeyed without argument, stretching out on the floor.

"Don't get any ideas about pressing that buzzer." The other man waved a magnum at both tellers.

"What's happening?" Holly's worried gaze was on her Uncle Jerry, who now lay on the floor like everyone else, except the tellers.

Joy put her hand on Holly's shoulder. "The bank is being robbed."

"What?" Holly looked at him, and he nodded.

"Move out of the way, gramps." The man with the handgun kicked Jerry in the ribs then slammed a bag on the counter. "Both of you fill this with everything you have."

The two tellers immediately began putting money into the bag. The one in front of the gunman reached for the silent alarm.

"Hey, I said stay away from that." The robber pointed the gun at the teller.

"He's going to shoot her!" Holly started forward then stopped. There was nothing she could do.

At that moment, Jerry yanked on the gunman's foot, sending him to the floor. Gunfire pierced the ceiling. The other man at the door aimed his weapon and pulled the trigger, shooting Jerry multiple times.

"No!" Holly turned her head away from where Jerry lay on the ground even as John and the manager ran up the hall.

The man near the door yelled. "Grab the money!" His partner yanked the bag from the teller even as the semi-automatic sprayed the hallway.

"Dad!" Holly flew to John.

Malcolm looked down as Joy gripped his arm, her fingers digging in hard. "It's so hard not to help when I know what to do."

Her words tugged at his conscience. This scene was mild compared to the many he'd worked as a Glasgow Watchman, but Joy was a healer, and it was probably traumatic for her even though she didn't know the victims.

He looked at Holly, tears tracked down her face as she knelt by John. "Dad? Dad? Please be okay."

Stealing himself against the softening of his heart, he waited.

The gunmen exited the front door and ran for their car. Still, no sirens could be heard. The thieves had done their homework. The local police department changed shift at two o'clock. It was a small department for a small rural town. By time they arrived, the suspects would be long gone and Jerry would bleed out.

"Dad?"

John started to get up, but his knee gave out and he rolled over grasping it. "Fuck." Taking a few deep breaths, he pulled himself up and hobbled over to Jerry. John dropped down next to his friend, despite the gory mess that had once been the man's back. "Anyone have medical training!"

Holly floated up and over to the counter where the date was posted for customers. She crossed her arms and spun back around to glare at him. "This is *not* going to happen."

He raised his brow. "Why not?"

"I won't let it." She took a furtive glance at Jerry. "I'll keep my dad and uncle from coming here and you can't stop me."

Malcolm nodded. "Then the teller will be dead instead."

She threw her hands up in the air. "Well, holy crap, what do you want me to do?"

Joy finally let go of his arm and took Holly by the shoulders. "Let's discuss this outside."

He followed the women as they phased through the roof.

Holly pulled away from Joy and advanced on him. "Why show me this? How am I supposed to change it?"

"I never said you were."

She poked her finger into his chest. "Listen, Mr. The World Sucks, you don't have to prove to me that life is tragic. Just tell me what I'm supposed to do about this."

He shrugged. "Why do you want to do anything about this?"

Her hand dropped, and she stared at him as if he'd just killed a hundred puppies. "Because that's my father who just got shot and my dear friend. I love them both to pieces. I don't want to see them hurt never mind killed."

"But you're in Scotland and they're here. How much can you really care?"

"Malcolm." Joy's stern tone wasn't going to stop him from driving his point home.

He raised his hands out to the sides. "You're over there because a man who is already dead means more to you than people who are still alive that you say you love."

Holly's mouth opened but nothing came out.

He pressed his advantage. "Oh, that's right, there's the One of a Kind Christmas Shop. That commercial endeavor must be more important than the people you love."

"That's enough!" Joy grabbed his hand, and before he could blink, they were racing through the ether.

Chapter Six

Within seconds they were in Joy's home, the pristine white walls a fitting backdrop for the rage she was in. If he'd wanted to see what lay beneath the surface of Joy Collingwood, he was seeing it now.

Solidifying, she turned on him. "What do you think you're doing? That was not what we were trying to achieve with that visit."

He looked down at his hand and ran his thumb across his fingers. "That's what I was hoping to achieve."

"Malcolm, showing her loved ones being shot is bad enough. You needed to let her come to her own conclusions."

He waved his hand to the side. "You heard her. She just wanted to change the outcome. She missed the meaning behind it."

"The meaning? You didn't even give the poor woman a chance to breathe, never mind process what she saw!" Joy patted her chest. "I'm still trying to process it, and I knew what was coming. Now, not only have you shocked Holly, but you've done exactly what Cameron said for you not to do. Do you wish to end your existence?"

She turned, stalking away from him then she spun back to face him. "How can I keep you safe when you do everything in your power to undermine me?"

He was so fascinated by this side of happy, caring Joy that it took a second to register what she said. "Keep me safe?" He not only sounded like a bumbling idiot, he felt like one too.

She rolled her eyes. "Of course! You're the one on trial here. You're the one, by your own words, being tested by those above Cameron. You're the one who chose me to come along for the ride. I assumed it meant you wanted my help, not that you wanted me to witness the end of your existence because if that's what you were hoping then you're sadly mistaken. I refuse to stand idly by while you destroy yourself."

Her anger took a toll on her hair, multiple strands now framed her face making her appear more wild and sexy then he'd given her credit for. Suddenly, the barbell jewelry seemed to fit, and his cock began to harden. He solidified as well. "Destroy myself?"

She stomped toward him, her ankle high boots clacking loudly on the tile floor of her living room. "That's what it looks like to me. What do you call it?"

Her blue eyes flashed, revealing emotions he hadn't seen since… since Blair. He brushed past her. He refused to go there again.

Her hands on his arm stopped him short.

"Where are you going? You owe me an explanation."

He scowled at the two hands holding his arm. He could easily break their hold. She thought she could stop him. Save him. He didn't need saving. He needed—

Like fog clearing beneath the onslaught of the sun, understanding dawned.

He needed her.

No. He shook his head. He didn't. He didn't need anyone. His gaze traveled up her arm to the pulse beating in her neck. His lips itched to lick her there, to move his hand under her dress and cup her between her legs to feel if the fuxing barbell lay there.

He forced his gaze to hers. The dark blue flecks in her eyes seemed to fight with the lighter colors, as if her body was on fire. As he stared at her, her mouth parted slightly, her breaths became more pronounced and her cheeks, already flushed with anger, grew rosier.

He'd have to be a saint to resist her. With his free hand, he grasped her behind her neck and brought her lips to within a hair's breadth of his. He held her there, hoping she'd try to pull away, silently begging her to tell him "no."

Once again, the photo of himself, tucked into her bedside drawer, flitted through his mind and he knew he was lost. With a groan, he pressed his lips to hers and breached her mouth with his tongue. He swept inside, dominating her, holding her there despite her hand gripping his arm.

When she sucked on his tongue, he gave up the fight. Within seconds, he'd phased them both and swept them together into her bedroom.

He wanted her. All of her. He angled them over her bed before solidifying them again, never letting go of her sweet mouth.

As soon as her body sunk into the mattress, she became more aggressive. She let go of his arm and ran her hand into his hair while her other hand burrowed beneath his cape to yank his shirt from the waistband of his kilt.

Her chest arched up against him and her legs spread, allowing his to anchor between them, his already hard cock pressing against her thigh. With a practiced hand, he unlinked his sporran and threw it to the side.

Her tongue explored his mouth, tangling with his own, and like her hands, it never stopped moving. The need she exhibited stoked his own.

Finally, he pulled his mouth away, anxious to taste her skin. She turned her head to the side, giving him access to her neck, which he gladly kissed.

Suddenly, she phased. "Disrobe me." At her words, he looked up, thinking she wanted him to strip her, but that wasn't the case.

She solidified again and beneath him now lay a naked Joy, and with her hand lifting his kilt and grabbing his ass, he had no doubt that she liked it this way. He pressed his abdomen against her thighs and she tilted her pelvis to rub herself against the course wool of his kilt.

He knelt back, not willing to let her climax so quickly. Despite his own need, the longer he could detain it, the sweeter it would be. Lowering his head, he nipped at each nipple, the hard points perfect for a piercing, but no jewelry shone there.

He sucked hard on each areola, holding it still while she writhed beneath him, her hands in his hair telling him she didn't want him to stop. But his curiosity was strong and he moved farther down, keeping his fingers on her hard nubs, just holding them, but not squeezing. If they were at his place, there was so much more he would do to her.

When he licked at her navel, the one place he was sure would be pierced, he swallowed his disappointment. Maybe the golden barbell was simply a wish and not something she actually had.

He finally pinched at her nipples in varying rhythms as he licked downward to her mons. The lack of hair anywhere there had his cock throbbing, anxious for release. There was no way he'd be able to do a complete investigation of her body. Again, if they were at his place…

He couldn't hold on anymore. Instead, he lifted himself over her and positioned his cock at her wet entrance. He rubbed his cock against her opening spreading her moisture over it and up. His tip hit against something hard and Joy let out a small yell.

His entire body tensed. Fux, the woman had a pierced clit! He lost all control and entered her in one hard thrust.

Joy saw stars as Malcolm's hard, thick cock pushed to his hilt, the reality shattering every fantasy about him she ever had. She opened her legs wider and bent her knees. As he pulled out, she tilted her pelvis for his next thrust.

His cock ran against her clit hood barbell, sending pleasure cascading through her to spike as he hit her cervix again. This is what she'd dreamed of. His abrasive peasant shirt rubbed against her nipples and his woolen kilt scraped against her inner thighs.

She forced her eyes open as he thrust again, his jaw was clenched and his silky black hair fell forward. Reaching up, she pulled his face toward hers.

At first, he resisted her tug, but she wouldn't let up as her need spiraled higher, his cock sliding along her clit and deep into her pussy. Finally, he let his head drop, and she thrust her tongue into his mouth. As soon as his met hers, she sucked, tensing the muscles in her sheath.

He exploded inside her.

Her entire insides burst into flame from her core outward, spiking up her spine and into her brain. Bliss, pure and white caught her in its sweet grip as she held on to the man that brought her there. He kept still, his own release filling her as he let her luxuriate in the pulses of sensation as they swept through her like wildfire.

At some point, she'd let go of his hair, so as she finally came down from her peak, she noticed his head turned away and over her shoulder. Her fingers still gripped his back through his shirt, so she reluctantly forced them to loosen. The man's back was like rock.

He lifted his head and stared at her.

She opened her heart, hoping for something sweet and wonderful.

"You have a clit piercing."

Her disappointment was fleeting and she chuckled, loving the way his eyes darkened as her sheath tightened around him with her movement. "Technically, my hood is pierced, but yes I do."

"I didn't expect that. Have all your lovers been as surprised as I am?"

She found the tension in his body odd for his question. "No, because I had it done after Alan broke it off with me. I went through that stage of hurt and rebellion and wanted to do something totally opposite of my character. I never had another lover after that, but…" She glanced toward her nightstand where she kept her sex toys. Would he find those exciting, too? Or think her pathetic?

His body relaxed as he looked at her nightstand as well. "You've enjoyed the jewelry anyway?"

She shrugged. "Maybe."

His gaze came back to rest on her, his weight firmly on his elbows now. "From what I just saw, I don't think the piercing opposite of your character at all."

"Thank you." She grinned. "I've always wondered how it would feel for a man. Did it feel okay to you?"

His grin turned devilish just before he ground his pelvis against her, sending sparks of excitement thrumming through her as he rubbed the little barbell against her nub. "It definitely adds something, but I think I need to test it more to be sure."

Sugar. He was more than just handsome, hard, and oh so heavenly. "Test it?" Her voice came out in a squeak.

His lids lowered as his eyes darkened again. "Aye. At my cottage. I have things I'd like to do to you there."

He hadn't moved an inch, but his words, along with his look, had her sheath tightening again. Was he getting hard already?

"Ah, lass, I canna take ye there yet."

She swore every muscle in her body melted into the ether at his brogue. It took her a moment to swallow against her suddenly dry throat. "No, you can't. We have work to do."

He shifted up, his cock still deep inside, but now his gaze rested on her breasts. "That can wait. Our time is our own."

She was about to argue that they had just shocked Holly and needed to follow-up on that, but his mouth came down on her breast and she forgot why that was important. Instead, she arched as he sucked hard, tonguing her nipple as she grasped the bedspread in her hands.

She was panting by time he released her hard nub, only to suck in her breath as he took her other between his teeth and tugged upward.

He finally let her other nipple go. "You were made for sex, Joy."

She heard his words and though her body reacted, her mind flinched. She tried to figure out why, but Malcolm had maneuvered his knees beneath her thighs without separating them and lifted her legs so her feet rested against his shoulders.

His hands ran from her ankles to her thighs before squeezing her legs against his chest. "Ye are bonnie fer sure, an' I'm needin' to feel ye against me." He phased. "Disrobe me." In an instance, his clothes disappeared and he was solid again.

She was left staring at a massively hard chest, broad shoulders and forearms larger than her biceps. "Oh, sugar."

He grinned. "Aye."

She took a deep breath, her whole body tingling just at the sight of him. "I never imagined you to be quite as large in person."

His grin froze and he glanced toward her other nightstand, or was he just looking away. He couldn't know about her photo of him, could he? She'd be mortified.

"I never imagined you to be so lively in bed."

She flushed, not entirely comfortable with a man discovering exactly how much she liked sex.

"Don't tell me you're embarrassed." His brow creased just slightly.

She reached up and tucked the stray hair that had fallen on her cheek back behind her ear. "It's been my very personal secret."

This time his grin turned devilish. "And glad I am ye shared with me. I wouldn't want ye any other way." He winked.

Her breath hitched as his cock inside her thickened even more.

Malcolm held out his hand. "Nipple clamps." A pair of gold nipple clamps connected by a heavy chain appeared in his hands. He held them for her to see. "I look forward to showing you the ones *I* have."

Her sheath tightened around him, and he lost his grin as his nostrils flared. Excitement skittered through her belly at his look.

Without a word, he attached a clamp to one breast and then the other, causing her heart to race. Then he tightened one until she moaned with arousal. Satisfied, he moved to the other, tightening it until once again she voiced her pleasure aloud.

He tugged on the heavy chain, and she closed her eyes as shocks traveled from her nipples to her core. "Nay lass, open yer eyes."

It was more the loosening of the tug on her nipples than his words that had her lifting her lids.

"That's better." He wrapped the chain around one of his large fingers and moved his hand above her chest before pulling upward.

"Yes. More." Her sheath tightened as he tugged her nipples higher, pleasure raging like a desert wash after a storm through her body. She arched her back, her elbows digging into the mattress, wanting even more.

He held her there, her body titillated more than any of her fantasies.

Then he started to move.

In her position, she could do no more than grab onto the sheets as he pulled his hips away before gliding back into her wet sheath. In this position, her barbell was exposed, but his cock didn't hit it and for that she was glad because one more stimuli and she'd come.

Malcolm pushed into her again, his movements deliberate, not frantic like the first time. His control now had her panting.

He set a tame rhythm, punctuating each slow thrust with a slight lift on the nipple chain. He played her like an instrument, as if he knew the shock from her nipples hit her core at the exact time his cock hit her cervix, creating a double spike in her need.

He held her there, gliding in and out, tugging and relaxing just a bit on the chain, watching her.

She dared not close her eyes, her instinct telling her this wasn't all he had for her.

When his free hand ran down one leg to the crease of her thigh, her stomach tensed. He tugged on the chain, arching her higher then his fingers moved across her belly and pressed as his cock sunk to its hilt. He slid back out and moved in again, only now his fingers pressed on her mons as he touched her cervix.

He glided out once more only to move back in as he tugged on the chain and his fingers pressed on her barbell.

She screeched with pleasure, her body wound up for her orgasm. This time the chain did not let up at all as he pulled away. She arched into the fingers against her clit, and they started to move in a circle just as his cock slid in with more force.

Her body burst into a million pieces like fireworks, the ecstasy bouncing throughout her like a pinball on steroids. She screamed, the pleasure needing a release.

Suddenly, the chain and nipple clamps disappeared and Malcolm was leaning over her, her knees against her chest and his cock pumping into her until he stilled, a low growl issuing from deep in his chest. As he flooded her sheath, her satisfaction was complete.

When he opened his eyes and looked down at her, he gave her a cocky grin. "You definitely need to come to my cottage."

Once again, it wasn't exactly what she was hoping to hear, but at least he was thinking of a future time for them…if he had a future. The sobering thought brought her focus back to their assignment.

She had to figure out a way to mitigate what he'd done to Holly or there would be no next time for them.

"You don't seem excited by that prospect." Malcolm's voice brought her gaze back to his, and he didn't seem too happy.

"Yes, I'd like that. I was just wondering how much time we have."

He gave her a skeptical sideways glance. "All the time we want."

She laid her hand against his cheek, and he jerked away. That was odd. She let her hand fall to his arm. "I mean after the way you treated Holly, I'm not sure how much time you have."

"It's not about my time." He looked away as he pulled his hips from hers and backed off the bed. "This is about our assignment. If what I did is what it takes to get Holly to face the facts, then that's what needs to be done." He stood at the foot of the bed and pointed to the left. "Your shower?"

She nodded, dumfounded by his statement.

He walked into the other room, his tight butt cheeks a continuation of the moving muscle in his thighs. His stride was purposeful, determined, and a shiver raced up her spine.

There was something about his attitude that reminded her of the military. She wished she could look at his life file. She held out her hand. "Show me Malcolm MacLachlan's life file." Once again, as expected, nothing happened.

She sat up and threw her legs over the side of the bed. Quickly, she padded out to her guest bathroom. She should be happier than an arch angel at having her fantasies about Malcolm fulfilled and then some, but instead, a feeling of dread hovered over her.

Malcolm finished his shower, ignoring the peppermint scented soap and calling for his own preferred evergreen. It was bad enough Joy's scent permeated his nostrils. After drying off, he dressed and headed out through the ether.

Everything about having sex with Joy had been a surprise,

from her passion to the emotions she caused inside him. Watchmen couldn't afford emotions. He needed to look at her objectively.

Too late for that to happen. If he wasn't careful she'd be making him think all was marshmallows and puppies. At least with their assignment that couldn't happen, at least not for Holly unless she made some serious changes.

What he'd said to Holly about her family in America was necessary. It was how he'd been trained to force change in others. What Cameron hoped to accomplish with their visit was riding on them making her see and feel again for other people beyond simple meddling.

He actually liked Holly, except for the blinders she wore when it came to her husband. If she thought seeing her adopted father being shot was hard, she was in for a rough ride.

He grinned. The woman did have back bone at least.

And Joy? He didn't like where they were headed. He thought he knew her type, the Pollyanna do-gooder who used to get in his way. Then she turned into a passionate vixen in bed just after claiming to protect him.

Maybe a visit to his cottage wasn't such a wise move.

The ether dissipated, and he found Joy already on the roof with Holly. She couldn't have arrived more than a few seconds before him.

As he floated toward them, he grimaced at Joy's words.

"Malcolm just wanted you to understand the true meaning behind this visit."

Holly pulled out of Joy's arms and nodded. "I do understand. While I'm in Deervale, I just assume that everything is okay back at home." She looked at him. "Am I supposed to move back to America?"

He shook his head. "You aren't supposed to do anything except learn from your visits."

Holly wiped her face with the sleeve of her sweater. "Can you at least tell me if they catch the thieves? Do they pay for their crimes?"

He looked at Joy, refusing to answer.

Joy frowned at him before responding. "I'm afraid not."

"What? People's lives are shattered and no one pays?" She crossed her arms. "How is that fair?"

"It's not." He grinned. "One reason I went rogue."

Holly's eyes lit with interest. "Rogue? What do you mean? Are you a rogue spirit?"

He laughed. "Hadn't thought about myself in quite that way, but maybe."

Joy was studying him far too intently.

He took Holly's hand. "I think we've spent enough time here."

Holly titled her head back to look at him. "Right now, the future is looking pretty bleak. Any chance there's something a little happier planned."

He waved his free hand toward Joy. "That's her department."

Joy didn't miss a beat as she floated to the other side of Holly and took her hand. "I think we can find more than one event in your future that will make you happy."

"Really? Excellent."

Joy whisked them upward and back toward Scotland.

As Joy led them on, her mind kept going back to Malcolm's strange pronouncement. Parts of his background were slowly coming together. She'd bet her entire cactus garden that he'd been in law enforcement simply by the way he'd viewed the bank robbery so dispassionately. It was far more than his gender that had him watching as if he were looking for clues.

He was either part of the Police Services of Scotland or from city law enforcement. Maybe detective or even forensics. That's what made his statement about going rogue so concerning, but if he was truly dangerous, he wouldn't be a spirit guide.

"Where are we going?" Holly's question brought her back to their trip, and she angled them a bit north.

"We're headed to the city of Inverness."

"Why?"

"There's someone you need to see there."

Holly's brow furrowed. "I don't know anyone in Inverness. Is this far in the future?"

"Not that far." She smiled. "We're going to a Christmas day gathering."

Malcolm, who'd been silent since leaving the bank, chose that moment to interject. "When was the last time you were at a Christmas day gathering?"

Holly looked away. "A few years ago, but last year I went to a Christmas Eve party that lasted all night."

Joy couldn't let the statement pass. After all, Cameron said not to be subtle. "But you left long before midnight."

"Well, yes. But that was because Cam had promised to come back and see me."

She caught Malcolm's raised eyebrows. Cameron visited Holly before and after Holly's time with her spirit guides? That was unusual. Joy was beginning to feel more confident in Malcolm's belief that they were all being used, but for what purpose? And what was her role supposed to be? If it was opposite of her usual role then she had no idea how to proceed, so until they figured it all out, she would stay the course.

She flew them along beautiful Loch Ness as it wound through the stone city. She loved the old feeling of it. Why had she never visited Scotland while she was alive?

Bringing them down to a two-story house in the middle of a row of them lined up along the street, she pulled them into the downstairs front parlor.

"Wow, you weren't kidding about this being a gathering. Look at all these people." Holly let go of their hands and floated to a corner of the room. "It's beautifully decorated. The tree in the front window has so many handmade ornaments." She laughed. "One of which is about to go into that toddler's mouth."

A young woman scooped up said baby and retrieved the ornament before it made it there. "Archie, I told you to move all the ornaments up on the tree," the woman yelled into the next room as she headed there.

Two young boys played with an electronic ball game in the middle of the floor, while three young teenage girls chatted in the corner. An old woman sat in the middle of a large comfy couch with a somewhat younger man on one side and another man about Holly's age on the other.

A woman a bit older than Holly entered the melee with a tray of cookies. "Granny, would you like some sweets to go with your tea?"

Malcolm floated between the young boys. "Do you see anyone you recognize?"

"Here?" Holly looked over each face then her gaze returned to the woman with the tray. "She looks familiar for some reason, but I don't know anyone this far north."

Joy cocked her head. "But you know people who live just west of here, right?"

Holly looked at her blankly for a moment before she remembered. "Cam's aunt and uncle. I can't believe I forgot about them. They raised him."

Malcolm drifted closer. "And the last time you visited with them?"

"You really have to spoil everything, don't you?" Her lower lip came out as she stared at him. Finally, she answered. "I visited them for Guy Fawkes night."

"What year?" Malcolm wasn't letting anything slide and in this instance, Joy agreed.

"Fine, it was a few years ago, with Cam. But I saw them at the funeral and that was only three years ago."

"Only?" Malcolm let his question hang in the air.

A sulking Holly wouldn't help anything, so Joy redirected her attention. "Who does the woman with the tray remind you of?"

Holly floated closer and stared. "Holy crap, she looks like Cam. Is this his half-sister?"

Holly's excitement was catching. "Yes!"

"All these people are part of her family and kind of related to Cam?"

Joy nodded.

Holly's awe turned into a giant smile. "I *have* to come visit."

"Not so fast." Malcolm's interjection caused Holly to roll her eyes.

Joy laughed. She much preferred guiding Holly with positive experiences rather than negative ones.

Malcolm had to be thick-skinned because he ignored both Holly's expression and her own laugh. "Why do you think Cameron's sister came to find you and then never knocked on your door?"

"You know about that?"

He nodded.

"I thought it might be bad news." Holly looked at Malcolm to see if she was right.

He shook his head. "No."

Holly grinned. "That's the happiest news you've given me since you showed up."

Joy bit her cheek to keep from laughing again.

Malcolm sighed before pointing to the man next to the grandmother. "That's the reason Lorna didn't knock on your door."

"Lorna." Holly said the name as if she were trying on a new

pair of shoes. "Lorna. That's pretty. I like it." She pointed. "Who is that and why did he stop her from visiting me?" Holly floated closer to have a good look at the man.

"He's Lorna's father." Malcolm paused then quirked his lip. "Not to give you more bad news, but he doesn't want Lorna to have anything to do with her biological mother's side of the family."

Holly spun at that. "Why not?"

Malcolm didn't say anything else, so Joy stepped in. "I imagine part of that is due to his current wife and part has something to do with his relationship with Cameron's mother, but any more than that, I can't tell you because I don't know."

Holly studied the man. He had orangey-red wavy hair that was sprinkled with a significant bit of white and thinning as well. His eyes were a grayish-blue and he sported a goatee that was all white.

Joy couldn't help but comment on Lorna's looks. "She has her father's coloring, but her mother's facial features and body."

"You know what Cam's mom looked like?" Holly floated higher to avoid being walked through as Cam's sister offered cookies to everyone.

Joy widened her eyes. "Don't you?"

Holly shook her head. "Cam didn't talk much about her because he was so young when she died. I don't think there are any photos of her."

Joy locked gazes with Malcolm. This was more cause for concern. Why hadn't Cam shared the photos with Holly? Were they not supposed to say anything, or did he want them to? The deeper they delved into this assignment, the more she felt as if she were walking through a mine field.

As if sensing her dilemma, Malcolm stepped in. "Your husband has pictures of his mom given to him by his aunt and uncle."

Holly's brow furrowed. "If he has them, then why did he never show them to me?"

Malcolm kept silent. Even Joy had nothing to offer as it would only be conjecture.

"Where are they?" Holly faced Malcolm.

Joy cringed. If Malcolm told, would Cameron's wrath cause him to lose his job? He already jeopardized it by telling her about them. Or was he supposed to because Cameron's superiors wanted him punished in some way? Or would the higher ups use Malcolm as a scapegoat, knowing his penchant for using shock and bad news to help his living clients.

She couldn't let him take all the blame, if that were coming. "I think you should ask Cameron that. You did say he will visit you later, right?"

Holly nodded, but she was clearly upset.

Maybe she shouldn't have mentioned Lorna's looks. "Lorna has a brother and a sister. Her sister is the one whose baby was about to eat the ornament."

"And that has to be her brother." Holly pointed to the young man on the other side of the grandmother.

"You're right." Joy moved next to the young man. "Of course, with his red hair, it wasn't that tough to figure out, was it?"

Holly's smile returned. "They all look so happy."

"It's Christmas day spent with family." Joy opened her arms wide. "What could be better?"

"Hogmanay." Malcolm's grin was mischievous.

"Oh no, I disagree." Holly shook her finger at Malcolm. "You Scots may like to celebrate the New Year, but I convinced Cam that Christmas was just as good."

Joy held her breath as Malcolm spoke. "From your actions over the last couple years, I wouldn't have known."

Holly's arms came across her chest. "I'll have you know I lost my husband. I've been grieving. Do you have any clue what that's like?"

Joy stiffened. *Oh, no.*

Malcolm's jaw tensed. "As a matter of fact, I do."

Holly didn't back down at all. "And what did you do? Did you go off partying with your friends? Celebrate Christmas with your family? You seem to know so much about what I should be doing. What did you do?"

"I killed people."

Chapter Seven

Joy stared in shock.

Holly's arms dropped as fear entered her eyes.

Before another word could be uttered, Joy grabbed Malcolm and brought him to the ether with no intention of bringing him out until he explained, but he took control of their flight and pulled them into a dark underground alley in a city somewhere.

She released him and set herself down at least twenty feet away before solidifying. She itched to ask him what he meant, but her tactics rarely worked. Instead, she waited.

Malcolm simply stared at her though she wasn't sure if he actually saw her. His hands were fisted and his body still.

There was a lone light over a door at one end of the alley and what looked like a couple of mechanized dumpsters of some sort, not that they helped since trash lay everywhere and from the movement of one pile, she'd bet there were plenty of rats. It was an unforgiving place.

"Welcome to Glasgow's underbelly, forty-five years in the future." Malcolm's voice surprised her, the tone almost sneering.

She returned her gaze to him. He'd solidified as well and had thrown his hood up over his head. Like that, with the backdrop of the darkness, he seemed sinister. *Is he?* Maybe that's why they were testing him. Maybe she'd be asked to report.

"Why did you bring us here?"

He opened his arms. "This was my life."

She widened her eyes. "You lived in an underground alley?"

His chuckle was harsh. "No. My home was far from here. This is where I worked. I was a Watchman. Trained to kill or take-in the criminal element, whichever was easier. Sanctioned by the city to clean it up." He gestured toward a dumpster. "Clean-up the human trash."

She shivered. Malcolm's normally dark eyes seemed to glitter with an amber light. "Is that what you meant when you said you killed people after your wife died."

He stepped closer to her as he shook his head. "My wife didn't die, though I hope she did soon after I did. It was Blair's death that sent me over the edge."

She should have known he'd have more than one love in his life. That bothered her for an irrational reason that she wasn't about to investigate now. "I think I'm confused."

"I'm sure you are. Allow me to enlighten you. I worked in this environment until Blair was shot. While she was with me, I had some semblance of what was normal. She was my consummate."

"What is that?" This is where she was having a hard time understanding.

He paused as if surprised by her question then he nodded. "A consummate is someone you commit to love for the rest of your life, a true soulmate. A wife is a person you plan to live with but you have no idea how long that will be. This was how it was set up in my lifetime since marriage among people of your lifetime stopped averaging more than ten years."

"Oh." That was a sad state. Maybe not marrying Alan had been a good thing after all. "So, Blair was your consummate and she was killed by…" she held out her hands, "this."

"Aye, this. This environment and my profession. It was the shooter's understanding of what I was that caused her death."

"A Watchman."

He looked beyond her as if she hadn't spoken. "He knew I had the right to kill him and he wasn't about to take that chance. As a Watchman, I wasn't allowed to hunt down criminals, only take them in or take them down as I came across them committing a crime. The shooter ran while I held Blair, lying to her and telling her she would be okay."

Joy wanted to take him in her arms and sooth away his pain, but instinct told her that was far beyond her ability.

"That night I resigned. I had a shooter to catch and no one was going to stand in my way."

She gasped. "You turned vigilante." Now she understood what he'd meant by saying he'd gone rogue.

At her words, his gaze came back to her. "I began wearing this cape to cover my face from all but the vermin I killed. It took me months, but I finally found the shooter. He was well aware of who I was before he died."

Joy took a step back. It was so at odds with her life and her time. She didn't understand it. She had lived helping the loved and treasured die, while he'd lived sending the hated and feared to their deaths.

Malcolm ignored her. "But my victory was hollow. Blair was still gone and without her, I'd lost all sense of what normal was. I slept all day so I could prowl these alleys at night for prey."

He blinked as if suddenly remembering where he was. His lip quirked up on one side, an odd look for what he'd told her. "I did bring the crime rate to its lowest level in history."

He shrugged. "I thought it ironic that I landed the job of Spirit of Christmas Future."

"Why?" She forced the word past her lips. Maybe it would help her understand him.

His eyes took on the glitter they had when he first started to speak. "Whenever a criminal sensed me lurking in the shadows, he would inevitably ask who was there. I always answered the same. 'Your future.' Others heard me on occasion, so they gave me the name of The Future."

The glitter dissipated and his grin was back. "Ironic, wouldn't you agree?"

She nodded, her throat too dry to speak. Suddenly, she didn't want the assignment anymore. Malcolm's pain was too deep and too wide. It threatened to swallow her though how that could happen, she didn't know.

She tried to smile in return, but her lips just wouldn't move.

"You asked if I wondered what happened after I died. I don't. I was set-up by my wife, Coira and the very people that live here." He spread his arms to encompass the dark alley. "I was shot, hung up by my wrists, then stabbed and left as a warning to others who wanted to clear the city of vermin. I bled out, but it took hours. I have no doubt those very vermin multiplied after I was gone."

The image he painted was so gruesome, his wife's betrayal so evil that her stomach started to rebel and bile crawled up her throat.

He sneered. "I bet it's the opposite for you. Tell me, Joy. How did you die?"

She shook her head, not really sure if he was still Malcolm or taken over by another entity.

"Oh, you must tell. I told you about my death, now tell me about yours." His eyes started to glitter again, and she instinctively stepped back. Was this how he interrogated suspects?

"Tell me!"

At his command, she opened her mouth. "My niece. She needed a kidney. I was a match. There were complications. I died." She choked the words out past her fear.

Malcolm's eyes lost their intensity. "And you want to know if she lived." The way he said it, in a sing-song voice made her sound pathetic. Compared to him, she was. Maybe she should just let it go.

He must have sensed her defeat. He waved his hand. "Go back to Holly. I'll be there shortly."

Not waiting another second, she flew upward, through the darkness of the underground alley, through the road above and out into the sun. She blinked to discover it was broad daylight.

Completely confused, she headed straight for Cameron's office.

Malcolm stared at the spot Joy had occupied. Having her in the darkened space was like having a flower in a dung heap —out of place. He'd wanted to shock her and he probably did, but he'd also surprised himself.

He looked around. This was where he'd lived, where his mind always drifted back to, but it wasn't where he belonged anymore. The realization was as confusing as it was true. This wasn't him. Joy's presence, her goodness, called to more of him than he thought was there.

Flying upward out of the catacombs of his old underground world, he felt lighter. He'd always thought his job as a Spirit Guide meant his life had been approved in some weird way, but it wasn't his life that was worthy, it was his soul.

He floated down outside his cottage not yet ready to return to their assignment. Solidifying, he wandered toward the sunlight just beyond his little valley. He'd hidden out here, far from the city, to avoid his new wife and those who would destroy The Future. He was glad he still had the pureness of the Scottish countryside to ease his mind.

He'd never completely trusted his wife. She'd begged him to take her with him after he'd killed her boss. The fear in her eyes had been real, but he had no doubt in hindsight that she was either afraid of him, or the man who had made her a spy.

Malcolm meandered along the burn of a small stream, the sunlight sparkling off the water as it followed itself down to the river beyond. Coira was like that, following whoever she thought was stronger. He felt no anger toward her. He'd known something wasn't right but had ignored his instincts, too focused on revenge. That she'd led him to his death at the hands of another crime chief was half his fault.

He stopped and threw his hood back to enjoy the sun in his re-creation of the Scottish hills. He'd had one woman he'd trusted with his life and she lost hers. He also had one woman he'd never trusted and he'd lost his. That begged the question of where Joy fit in.

It wasn't as if his life was in danger, though she did think he'd cease to exist if he angered the wrong people. *How can I keep you safe when you do everything in your power to undermine me?* Her words echoed in his mind. She sincerely thought his existence was in danger, but his gut, his instinct, was telling him that wasn't the case.

He walked toward the ancient circle of stones and leaned on the closest one. If his gut was right, he was safe. Holly was also safe as she was among the living. That left only two possible people in danger, Joy and Cameron.

A spike of fear shot up his spine at the idea that Joy could be the target. Did Cameron's superiors know that he would choose Joy as his partner? He tried to think back on every interaction he'd had with her. When viewed in its entirety and without the larger picture, it was obvious he'd pick her.

But when he compared it with the other spirits he'd met with, his choice of Joy appeared to be out of the blue, which was in fact, Cameron's reaction. But Cameron was being manipulated as well. It wasn't hard to figure out that in order for Cameron to help his wife, he had to do things he didn't want to.

Malcolm grinned. Cameron would never have chosen him to help Holly if he'd had a choice.

Did that mean Cameron's existence was in jeopardy? He found that hard to believe, but wouldn't rule it out any more than he'd rule out Joy's danger. He simply didn't have enough information.

He held out his hand. "Joy Collingwood's life file." As he expected, nothing happened. He didn't need Cameron's since he'd watched the complete file of Cameron and Holly's life up until Coco and Ian had left. He could think of only one way to make Cameron reveal what was going on and that was through Holly.

Standing upright again, he patted the warm stone behind him. "Thanks." A vibration pulsed against his hand, and he smiled. With a new goal in mind, he breathed easier.

Phasing, he flew to Holly at Lorna's family Christmas. At least with his new goal, he wouldn't be so much at odds with Joy, which meant that a visit to his cottage was back on the table.

He arrived only a second after he left, but Joy wasn't there. That surprised him. He'd expected her to be reassuring Holly by now. It was probably better if he handled Holly anyway after the shock he'd given her.

Holly's voice was barely a whisper. "You killed people?" She floated backwards.

He waved off the statement, not willing to tell her the whole truth. "I was part of a special force within the department of police."

She halted. "Like a SWAT team or something?"

"Or something."

"In other words, you were so devastated that you didn't think your life worth living and risked getting killed in the line of duty." From her shrewd look, she assumed she had him all figured out.

"No. I didn't take any unnecessary risks." *Except marrying Coira.* He shook his head. "I was too busy hunting down the man who killed the woman I loved."

Holly's gaze softened, sympathy written all over her face.

Schitz, not again. "I had a mission. What's yours?"

Holly's eyes widened. "Mine?" She snorted. "You mean like hunting down the man who killed my husband? That might be a little difficult since Cam did that all by himself."

He wanted her to get angry at her late husband. As far as he could see, it was the only way that she'd finally let go of him. Was that what Cameron's superiors wanted?

Holly scowled, but the hurt in her dark chocolate eyes still held sway.

He pressed her. "Did Ethan try to stop Cameron and Brody from rock climbing on that Christmas day?"

Pain filled her eyes. "He did, but they only listened to him half the time. Cam had new equipment he wanted to try out. He was too impatient to wait for the mist to clear. Ethan tried to warn him it wouldn't be just wet, but icy."

"Do I have this right? Cameron left you on Christmas day to try out new rock climbing equipment even though Ethan warned him it was dangerous?"

Holly's brows lowered. "Yes." She crossed her arms. "If he'd just stayed home with me like we always did, having Brody and Ethan over for dinner, he'd still be alive today."

"That means he died for no reason than his own need for an adrenaline rush and good time, when he could have been home with you. Climbing was more important than having the rest of his life with you."

"Yes. No. Cam loved me."

She was steadfast in her belief in Cameron, which was admirable but not helping her. "But if he'd stayed home, you might even have a couple of children by now. It's been three years."

Holly threw her arms up, her scowl at odds with the tears in her eyes. "Hey, that's who he was. Even now he feels so guilty about that."

Ah, now that was a revelation. Cameron's motivation in helping

Holly was his own guilt. It had to be pretty powerful for him to beg for, and receive, a special dispensation to be allowed to affect her life. And what were the terms of that boon?

Holly's expression turned smug. "In fact, if he didn't feel so bad about that, you wouldn't be here right now."

He swallowed a laugh. Cameron's wife was definitely not a pushover. "If I wasn't here, I'd be helping another person, probably someone who was willing to accept help."

"Hey, wait a minute. I'm willing to be helped. I think it's you who doesn't want to be helped."

That didn't make sense at all, so he ignored her statement. "But this isn't about me. I obviously continued to live and make a difference in other people's lives. What are you doing?"

"I'm doing a lot. I have the shop which makes many people happy. I've hired Cameron's cousin Brooke to help me there, and she loves it. I also, well, I participate in the community."

He raised his brow.

"Don't give me that look." Holly looked beyond him. "Where's Joy? She was just here a minute ago."

That was a good question. She could join them at any time. So why wasn't she back?

~~*~~

Joy paced the confines of Cameron's office. She'd popped in at multiple times and each time he wasn't there. For the first time, she wished she knew where he existed in his off hours. How could he not be working for so many days and times? It didn't make sense.

She stopped. *I'm simply treading carefully. Cameron is being manipulated as are we. If we don't get this right, there will be dire consequences.* Malcolm's words from earlier froze her to the spot.

What if Cameron wasn't available only to her? Maybe the answers she wanted on Malcolm, she wasn't supposed to get from

Cameron. Then from who? She was denied his life file and denied her boss' counsel. Who else could she ask about his worthiness? His trainer?

She looked around the office as if it could somehow tell her what she should do next. Everything was in its proper place, Cameron's desk completely clear. She moved toward the chair she usually sat in then changed her mind and leaned against the desk like Cameron always did.

"Who am I supposed to ask?"

At her words, the shadow of a figure appeared, leaning against the wall to her right. She snapped her head around, but it disappeared. Sugar, who was it? Who leaned against the wall— "Oh."

She stood. She had to ask Malcolm himself. Cameron's hint drifted through her mind. *Don't be subtle.* Did he mean with Holly or Malcolm? Was her assignment both of them like she'd originally thought?

And why couldn't someone just tell her what she was supposed to do instead of making it a stinking guessing game? "Okay, fine. I'll confront Malcolm and Holly both, but if that's not what you wanted, you better tell me soon, or I'm not responsible for what happens."

The room was silent and nothing moved. She'd half hoped that a file drawer would pop open or a scene would play before her, but that would be far too obvious. Sighing, she phased and sped back to Inverness. She could be there a second after she'd left.

As she came into the house, she frowned to see Malcolm and Holly watching the family exit the room for dinner. She must have miscalculated her time. Was Holly okay?

"Glad you didn't move on without me." She gave them a smile.

Malcolm looked relieved, which told her something wasn't right.

"We wouldn't leave without you." Holly faced her. "My guess is Malcolm will want to take me some place depressing next, and there's no way I'll go there without you."

Cameron's wife was pretty sharp. "I don't think Malcolm would be so crass as to leave without me, but since you bring it up, should we move on?"

Holly gave Malcolm an odd look. "That's what I'm supposed to do, I guess."

He nodded. "Aye. Take my hand." As he took Holly's hand, he gave her a challenging look.

She nodded regally. What? Did he think she was afraid of him after what he showed her of his life? She may not have experienced what he did, but she had strength he didn't even know about. Determinedly, she grasped his hand. He wouldn't be so smug if he knew she planned to drill him about it.

He grinned and gave her hand a squeeze. "Back to Deervale."

She frowned at him. How could he be so happy when their next visit was so sad. Or was he smiling about something else? She leaned in to whisper. "You'll have to tell me how you explained your killing statement to Holly."

His grin didn't leave his face. "I'll be happy to."

There was definitely something else going on. He looked like a dragon who'd just fired an entire town. If he suddenly started breathing fire, she'd grab Holly and escape.

He turned back to steer them in the right direction, and she studied his profile. His face was perfectly sculpted even from the side. His jaw was strong and rugged, darkened as it was by his rough goatee. His nose was straight and his cheek bone angular. Dragon or not, she had to admit, he was very hot.

At her thought, her body heated. That's the last thing she should be thinking about. She should be planning her interrogation of said dragon. Malcolm had been well trained to elicit the truth from people he questioned. Though his methods were effective, they weren't her way. There was more than one way to skin a cat, or a dragon.

"That's Brody and Sarah's house." Holly pointed to a stone home on a street off the main road of town. "Brody and Cameron were so much alike, I can't believe Ethan put up with the both of them."

Joy looked around Malcolm to catch Holly's eye. "I'm betting you helped even the odds a bit."

Holly laughed. "You're right. I don't know how many times Brody and Cam suggested some crazy venture and Ethan and I argued against it. I think we all balanced each other out. Brody and Cam took a few less risks and Ethan and I lived a little wilder than we would have because of them."

"And then Brody's girlfriend Sarah joined you. Where did she fit in?" Malcolm's entrance into the conversation had them hovering over the house.

"Oh, she was our mediator. She's very gentle and practical. She and Brody have what Cam and I had. They're married now. Sometimes though, it's hard to watch them together. I'm so happy she hasn't had to go through what I have yet."

Joy's heart squeezed. "What do you mean 'yet'?"

Holly, still holding Malcolm's hand, floated around to face her. "Brody is so much like Cam, taking risks he doesn't need to. I'm afraid he'll do what Cam did and leave Sarah a widow like me."

Joy couldn't resist. She laid her hand on Holly's cheek. "You don't have to worry about that. Brody learned from Cameron's mistake. He won't be taking unnecessary risks."

Holly's brows lowered in concern. "But the Brody I know doesn't seem any different." Her gaze moved to Malcolm. "And I would know because I do go to their house once in a while. In fact, I'll be at their Christmas Eve party again tonight."

Joy had a feeling Malcolm was ready to respond in the same way she would, but it was past time to stop making Malcolm look like the bad spirit. He'd had enough of the bad in his life. "But you aren't around them nearly as much as you used to be. I'm thinking four times a year hardly qualifies you to make a judgment on Brody's behaviors. Do you?"

Holly's gaze snapped back to her in surprise. "I guess you're right. Like I said, it can be hard to see them together. They love each other so much. Like I loved Cam."

"Then I suggest we go inside." As Malcolm spoke, he pulled them both through the roof and down to the first floor where Sarah sat in a recliner. She was dressed in silky pajamas despite the fact it was midday. She stared at the cold fireplace, a lifeless look in her eyes.

Joy's stomach clenched, and she let go of Holly's hand.

"Why does she look so sad?" Holly drifted over to Sarah.

"I've made some mince and tatties, Sarah. Want to come in and eat?" Brody strode into the room, as loud and joyful as ever.

The young woman didn't respond.

Brody knelt down next to her. "Come on, dove. You need to eat. You need to stay healthy."

Sarah turned her head. "But I'm not hungry."

Brody took her hand. "I know, but eat for me. It's been a couple months and we said we'd try again next month. You're going to need to be in tiptop shape."

Holly looked up at Malcolm. "Try again? Are they trying to get pregnant?"

He shook his head. "No. They were pregnant."

"Oh, no." Holly's eyes watered. "Sarah always wanted to be a mom. She said she might as well have a baby since she was already taking care of Brody." Holly turned to watch the couple.

Sarah looked at Brody. "But I'm afraid. What if it happens again? I couldn't bear it."

Brody pulled her up to stand and held her close. "I know. If you don't want to try, we can adopt."

Sarah pulled back to stare at him. "Adopt?"

He nodded. "I know you'll make a wonderful mother. You have so much love to give. Whether it's from us or a child who needs a home, I don't care. I just want you to be happy again."

Sarah turned her head away. "I'm sorry. I've been such a terrible wife to you lately."

Brody took her chin in his hand and turned her back to look in his eyes. "You could never be a terrible wife. The fact you put up with me at all proves what an amazing woman you are. I hate to see you so sad. I just want you to be happy."

"I love you so much, Brody."

He took his wife in his arms and held her close. His own eyes watering.

Joy felt her heart breaking, knowing she needed to drive home what past spirits already told Holly, but then Malcolm took her hand, his eyes asking her if she wanted him to do what needed to be done.

Silently, she shook her head and straightened her shoulders. He wasn't the only one with backbone here. "Sarah and Brody lost their baby after five months. It was devastating for them. But they will try again. They can't stop living because someone they loved with all their hearts is gone."

Holly, who had turned away from the couple when Joy started speaking, shook her head. "But I didn't even have a chance to have a baby with Cameron."

"And I never had a chance to become pregnant because it was impossible for me. I know it's no comfort, but for every heartbreak we each have, someone else has it worse."

Holly's bottom lip jutted out. "I understand that with my head, but it doesn't help my heart."

Malcolm interjected. "Then maybe your heart needs to focus on other people."

"You mean like Sarah and Sophia?"

Joy could tell Malcolm wanted to elaborate, so she quickly let go of his hand and wrapped her arm around Holly's shoulders, anxious to show a united front. "That could be, but there are so many possibilities. Just like Sarah, you are capable of loving many people."

Holly perked up a bit. "Like Mom and John."

"Yes, and even more, maybe even people you haven't met yet. It doesn't mean Cameron won't always hold a piece of your heart. He will, but you have so much more love to give and a lifetime ahead of you. You need to embrace those possibilities and loosen your hold on the past."

"Again, I understand what you're saying, but—"

"I think we should watch more with Brody and Sarah." Malcolm pointed to the couple who were passing through the doorway into their dining room.

Holly nodded and followed.

Confused, Joy looked at Malcolm. There wasn't anything else that could help Holly here.

He grasped her hand and swept her into the ether. When it parted, they were back inside his cottage.

Since he solidified, she did as well. "Is something wrong?"

He let go of her hand. "Aye, there is. I need to do something right now."

"What?"

His eyes had darkened as he stared into hers, and shivers of anticipation raced through her.

Chapter Eight

Malcolm still held her hand but his other came up to cup her face. The second his fingers touched her ear, an electrical shock hit her.

She jumped back, holding the side of her face. "Ouch! That hurt."

He fisted his hand as well. "What the fux?"

She giggled. "Fux?"

His brow was still lowered in anger. "Yeah, it's a swear word in my time."

He lifted his hand to touch her face again, and she backed away. "Sorry, I'm not into pain."

He dropped his hand. "I'm trying to discover what the problem is. Give me your hand."

Since they had held hands coming in to his cottage, she allowed him to take hers again.

"Now give me your other one."

Seeing no harm in that, she lifted her hand to his, but the second they touched, another shock hit. "Ouch. Okay, no more experimenting. Your cottage is alive with electricity." She looked at one of the chairs that conformed to a person's body. "It must be in this future setting."

Malcolm's brows were still lowered, but he nodded. "For some reason when we touch in more than one place, it completes some kind of a circuit. I can't tell you how much that frustrates me."

"Why?" Because he wanted to kiss her?

"Never mind. It doesn't matter since my house is somehow wired." He grinned, the look in his eye calculating. "If it's this future time setting, then I know the perfect spot." Without asking, he grabbed her hand and pulled her outside.

The view of the two mountains surrounding his cottage was breathtaking. She barely paid attention to where she was walking as she looked behind them. The mist reflected the green of the grass on the inclines, giving the little valley a faerie feel as they walked in the shadow of the mountains.

When sunlight hit her head, she finally looked to where they were headed. "Oh." In front of them was a field of standing stones. They were very old and there didn't appear to be any particular order, but with the sun shining brightly, she could almost imagine them as chest pieces of long ago giants.

Malcolm brought her a few yards into the field then stopped and turned her toward him. He grasped her other hand and smirked. "As I expected. We can't find any older ground than this without going back in time."

It took her a moment to understand what he meant, but as his hand left hers and cupped her cheek with no electric shock, she understood.

"I ken what ye did fer me at Brody's."

Oh sugar. When he used that brogue, she wanted to snuggle up to him and never leave. Never? She stiffened at the thought, but Malcolm's lips were already upon hers and her concentration scattered.

The kiss was different. It wasn't rushed passion. It was sensual, leisurely and made her knees weak with anticipation. Wrapping her arms around his neck, she leaned in to him, fisting the hood behind his neck as his tongue enjoyed her mouth.

One of his arms held her tight to him, while his other hand pressed her against his growing erection.

His mouth left hers to lick the pulse at the side of her neck. When he brought his lips to her earlobe, she giggled, pressing her shoulder up toward her head to stop him. "I'm ticklish there."

He stared at her as if he'd never heard of that before, but then his gaze softened. "I'll try to avoid that area then. Are there any other ticklish places I should know about?"

She flushed as she shook her head.

"Good, because I dinna wanna miss one inch of yer skin."

Now it was more than just her cheeks that were warm.

Malcolm unclasped her arms from his neck and stepped away. He unhooked his cape and with a flourish set it on the ground in the shade of the standing stone next to him. When he stood again, he looked right at her as he phased. "Disrobe me."

She sucked in her breath. Malcolm stood there solid again, legs braced apart, his fists at his waist as if he were ready for battle, except he was from the future and he wore no clothes. And that's what made him so impressive. His chest looked as hard as the stones surrounding them, its mounded perfection like the mountains near his home. His shoulders were broad and thick with muscle that continued down his arms like waves melding into one another.

His thighs were larger than her head and as ripped as his abdominals. Sticking out in hard relief between them was his cock. The veins beneath the skin meandered their way around and up toward the large tip.

She brought her gaze upward, past his thick neck, beyond the dark scruff of his chin, to find his gaze intent. Instinctively, she phased.

"Disrobe her."

Joy immediately solidified again to feel the heat of the sun on her body as her clothes vanished. She wasn't unhappy with her body, but standing naked outdoors was a new experience, especially with the man of her dreams staring at her.

No, not staring…appreciating.

His gazed moved slowly over her, a slight smile on his lips. When he reached her feet, he took his time perusing her, especially at the juncture of her thighs and her breasts. Finally, his eyes locked with hers.

She felt frozen in place by his look. There was desire and something more that had her heart hoping.

"Release her hair."

Her hair fell against her back, a sensation she wasn't used to. Unless she were washing and drying it, she always kept it in a low bun at the back of her head. Its soft weight against her skin made her feel vulnerable and delicate.

Malcolm lifted one hand toward her, and she put hers in it. Pulling her toward him, he held her in his embrace, her soft body molding against his hard one. "Joy."

He said her name with such reverence as if she and its definition were one in the same. "You're different from anyone I've met, living or spirit." That he stopped using his brogue had her paying close attention. "I'm glad I chose you as my partner on this journey."

There was more meaning behind his words, but she didn't know him well enough to understand. What she did understand was that something had changed for him, something for the good.

She lifted her hand to his face. "I'm glad you chose me, too. I've already learned so much about myself and about you."

He turned his face toward her palm, but instead of the erotic lick she expected, he kissed it. "Lay with me?"

He didn't need to ask. It was obvious she was incredibly attracted to him. They'd already had amazing sex, but something in his tone told her this would be different. She smiled shyly. "Yes."

His answering smile had no glimmer of seduction in it. It was purely happy, and her heart grew fuller.

Malcolm laid her down on his cape, facing the monolith that kept them out of the heat of the sun. He knelt on one knee beside her and picking up her hand, he kissed her fingers, each one getting its own brush of his lips. Then he moved to her palm, then her wrist and methodically made his way up her arm.

She felt worshiped as if she were some pagan goddess, and he some druid priest sent to make a sacrifice to her. She pushed the thought away. She was no goddess and she sincerely hoped there'd be no sacrifices required from either of them.

When he'd made it to her shoulder, he leaned over and kissed her gently, not breaching her lips. The whole action made her feel beautiful and cared for at the same time.

He moved away to kneel at her feet. He lifted one foot and kissed her arch, her ankle, her knee. He really did mean to kiss every inch of her.

Malcolm inhaled as he kissed Joy's sweet skin. Some time between starting their assignment together and now, he'd become addicted to peppermint. He hadn't expected that. Then again, Joy had been a bundle of surprises. From her secret jewelry to her failed engagement to her worry for him, she'd been far more than he'd expected.

That she'd taken on his role as interrogator at Brody's had been a defining moment for him. Unlike Blair, Joy wasn't a pushover, doing what had to be done, so he wouldn't be the only one urging Holly along. And unlike Coira, she was honest despite her habit of suppressing her reactions to hide the depth of her feelings.

Joy was far more than puppies and marshmallows and if that were true, it meant he had the chance to be more than locusts and rain. It was that possibility that had him giving her the experience she deserved.

As he kissed her inner thigh, he had to thank whoever set up the shocks at his cottage because there he'd be tempted to use the many devices at his disposal. Here, among the stones, they could return to the elemental experience of a man taking his woman.

His woman?

Maybe not his, but as he kissed the hard nub at the apex of her thighs, definitely woman. He continued his kisses over her belly, enjoying the fluttering that played across it. He moved to her ribs and true to her word, she wasn't ticklish there. When he reached her full breasts, he forced himself to featherlight kisses despite the hardness of her nipples.

He ran his kisses over her collar bone, along her jaw, on her cheek, eyebrows and nose, until he reached her forehead and her hairline. Her hair sprawled out above her, and with his weight on his elbows, he let his face fall into the rich silky waves. He breathed deeply.

His lungs filled with the scent of peppermint and a sweet essence that was pure Joy. Her hands came up to lightly rest on his back as she turned her head and kissed his neck. He pulled back to gaze into her turquoise eyes. "You are bliss itself."

"And you are a dream come true."

At her response, he remembered the photo of himself tucked away in her drawer. He had to know. "Have you dreamed about me?"

He expected her to look away, but she didn't. "I have."

For a moment, he forgot to breath. "Why?" He couldn't see any possible reason for her to dream about him. They'd barely said a few words in passing. They had different philosophies. They were from completely different countries and time periods.

She ran her hand through his hair, sending hot need racing down his back. "Because something about you calls to me."

"Like a moth to a flame?" He quirked his lip up.

She shook her head. "No. Like the flower turns to the sun or a river seeks the ocean. I can't explain it any other way."

Was that why he'd chosen her to work with? Was there an

unconscious need on his part as well, and he simply didn't recognize it? It was something to ponder, but not now. Not while he had her in his arms.

"Kiss me." Joy's breathless words were more a command than a request, and he was happy to comply.

Taking her lips with his again, he swept his tongue between them and tasted her.

She grasped him tighter as her tongue played with his, retreating then beckoning, at once submissive yet dominant and everything in between. That was Joy.

He held her as long as he could, enjoying her mouth with his own, but his cock had been denied too long and demanded attention. Last time he had her, he couldn't wait, but this time it was her choice, her speed.

He broke their kiss and pulled himself away to rest his back against the monolith shading them. He grasped her hands and pulled her to a sitting position, her knees bent over his calves.

She smiled. "You read my mind."

Happy to have pleased her, he opened his arms. "Do with me as ye will, lass."

Her gaze softened before she scooted herself up onto his legs, her moisture leaving a light sheen on one of thighs. His hard cock stood up between them, but she made no move to lower herself onto it. Instead, she leaned forward and took one of his nipples between her lips and sucked.

The fission went from his chest to his groin at lightning speed, and he sucked in his breath. Her teeth rolled his nipple before biting it lightly. Schitz, if she kept that up, he'd never last.

Maybe she needed a bit more encouragement. He moved his hand to the moisture between her legs and flicked her barbell with his finger.

"Oh." She rose up.

That little piece of jewelry would be his saving grace. As she leaned in to play with his other nipple, he flicked the barbell again. Again, she came off his lap and let go of him.

She stared at him a moment, trying to figure out what he wanted.

"I need ye, woman." He barely kept the growl from his voice.

She gave him an impish smile before rising up above him. "Now?"

Her innocent look was in stark contrast to her hardened nipples and her flushed cheeks.

"Aye, now." Despite the urge, he kept his hip from thrusting upward, forcing himself to remain in place as her moist opening covered his tip.

He set his jaw, determined to let her find her own pace. Luckily, Joy was as excited as he was.

Slowly, she glided down the length of him until she was fully seated. She angled her pelvis toward him, bringing her luscious breast to his face.

The invitation was too blatant to resist, and he latched on to the hard nipple and sucked. He grasped her nub between his teeth and held it, forcing her to pull against him when she rocked away. That she liked it was obvious in her tightening sheath.

"Oh yes." Joy grasped his shoulders as she rocked her hips back and forth grinding against him.

Soon she was lost to the sensations of her barbell rubbing against him and her clit while he stayed still, letting her take her pleasure as she liked.

At her yell, he had to let go of her breast to clench his jaw, determined to let her have her complete fulfillment. There was something about watching a woman exploding with ecstasy around him that he'd always found to be the most intimate of situations.

She at her most vulnerable, and he basking in her pleasure,

glorying in his ability to give her that. To have the experience with Joy was…unexpected. Doubt crept into his mind, trying to steal these few blissful moments, so he shoved it aside.

Joy fell against him, her head on his shoulder, her breathing rough.

He held her gently, loving the feel of her long hair against his skin. When her breathing finally calmed, she leaned back, causing him to groan at the added friction.

"You didn't orgasm?" Her eyes were wide.

"No, I wanted to watch you."

She opened her mouth, but nothing came out.

He chuckled then wished he hadn't as it moved his cock inside her tight sheath. "If you would like to reach fulfillment again, I suggest turning around."

She looked behind her as if he meant she would see something then her breath caught as her sheath tightened. "Oh."

He clenched his teeth at the sensation, not sure he would be able to wait, but willing to try.

Slowly, she slid off his cock, stretching his control, but once the cooler air hit, he gathered air into his lungs again and sat straighter while she positioned herself over him once more, this time facing away from him. She sat down fast, spearing herself on his cock and sending a spike of need tightening his balls.

Joy looked at him over her shoulder. "Sorry."

He shook his head, his jaw still clenched. Taking slow deep breaths, he eventually found some semblance of control, though not much.

"I've never done it this way. What do I do?"

He wrapped his arm around her waist. "Just move up and down and enjoy."

She looked at him over her shoulder and winked. "That I can do."

He sucked in another deep breath at the excitement in her eyes before she turned away again. Fux, he wouldn't last. Before she could start, he moved his hand down to her clit and rubbed his finger against it. Her sheath immediately tightened.

With his other hand, he cupped her breast and used his fingers to tweak her nipple. Again, her sheath tightened.

"I don't think this will be very long." Her words were whispered in worried tones.

"I'm ready when you are." *More than ready.*

She leveraged herself up and glided back down. Her sheath sucked at his length as his finger rubbed against her barbell. He buried his face in her hair, the scent of peppermint more enticing than before.

She moved again, and he held his breath, trying to keep his orgasm at bay. Finding her rhythm, she kept a methodic pace that gradually increased. High-pitched moans left her throat with each downward movement.

He forced himself to focus on her body, but the pulsing within her sheath pulled him closer to letting go. Just when he thought he'd failed, her sheath squeezed and she yelled.

"Malcolm!"

His body shuddered as his hips thrust upward, unable to control his actions. He grasped her breast in one hand and pressed her pelvis tightly to him, his cock pumping out his pleasure, filling her.

His head fell back against the stone as his own yell left him.

He remained like that as his breathing slowed and his body calmed, but at the vibration against his back, he groaned.

As much as he'd enjoyed being with Joy, it was time to return to work and discuss their final visits. He couldn't tell her what he planned, or she'd stop him. His gut said he was right and the only way to help Cameron was to put him in the middle of everything.

Joy leaned back against him, the scent of their lovemaking

urging him to forget about their task a little longer, but he wanted it done and over.

"If I wasn't already here, I'd think I'd died and gone to heaven." At her giggle, her sheath pulsed against him.

He would be hard in a matter of seconds, if he didn't get them back to their assignment. "Unfortunately, we have a job still to do."

She sighed. "You're right. I may be happy, but Holly isn't. I think she's even more confused about what she should do."

"I agree."

Joy sighed one more time before finally lifting herself off him. It took all his willpower not to grab her and force her to stay. Now that was odd. They hadn't even had the kinky sex he'd hoped for.

Either he was losing his touch or he'd lost his objectivity. *Objectivity.*

Joy sat next to his legs, her own out to the side, ever the proper miss, but as naked as she was, he had no hope of concentrating.

He phased. "Return clothes." As soon as he was dressed again, he solidified.

"Oh, you're no fun." Joy frowned before she followed suit.

He quirked his lip. "We'll focus better this way."

"I know." She smoothed out the edges of her green dress. "Do you still agree that we show Holly what's in store for Ethan and then the two possibilities for her?"

"No." At his answer, her attention turned back to him. "I think Holly's two possible futures should come first. Since we've started with her, the probabilities have gone down on both."

"You really can see the probabilities of each?" Her eyes widened with admiration.

He smiled. "You obviously haven't worked with anyone from the future before. Yes, I can tell *exactly* which future has the highest probability."

Joy's brows lowered. "So, at the hospital, when you said Thea dying was the most likely scenario, you actually based that on what you could see?"

The urge to reassure her wouldn't be denied. He was so far from objective on this case, if he was still alive, he would be fired. "Yes, but the probabilities of others are based on how things stand before we start the visit." He paused. Did Cameron's bosses understand that?

"And?"

At her prompt, he continued. "But the probabilities on Holly herself, shift depending on how she's feeling and what she's learning."

"That's odd. I wonder if we're helping or hurting. I've never had a case as complicated as this one." She pushed her hair behind her ear, revealing her concern and that she'd forgotten her hair was down.

"You mean in regards to our superiors meddling with it?" He grimaced, not happy about that himself.

"Yes." Joy scowled. "I hope the powers-that-be don't want us to hurt Holly. I just can't do that."

He understood her concern. He liked Holly as well and was pleased she was strong enough to take everything they'd thrown at her so far.

Joy laid her hand on his bare knee, sending his thoughts in a different direction all together. "Why do you want to switch the order of the visits?"

He crossed his legs at his ankles to dislodge her hand so he could focus. She was too tempting. "I think we should hold off visiting Ethan. I want to see if she remembers to ask about what happens to him in the future. If she doesn't, we can, of course, suggest him, but I think it will give us a good idea of how far she's come in thinking of others, beyond the simple daily life events."

Joy smiled, her eyes sparkling with excitement. "That's a wonderful idea."

He nodded once. "Thank you."

Her laugh permeated his body and settled into his heart. "I have to admit, I can't wait to see how Holly reacts to seeing herself in the future. Which would you like to take, the happy Holly or the grumpy Holly?"

She obviously thought the first would be easier, but he had a feeling both would be difficult for Holly, especially because they each were less than forty percent probable, which meant Holly's emotions were in flux. "You can choose."

She appeared to think about it seriously. "Hmm, I'll take the grumpy Holly as I think it will be easier to sway her away from it. Besides, you should get to show her a happy event. Maybe this way, Cameron will see that you've changed your ways."

From her concerned look, he had the feeling she was more worried about him than Holly, but he'd grown more and more confident that this wasn't about him. "I agree with you that your visit will be easier to talk to her about."

When she continued to look distracted, he recalled she'd been late to the last visit, which was an impossibility considering their ability to travel through space and time. "Where did you go after you left me in Glasgow?"

Her gaze snapped to his before sliding away. "I went to find Cameron. I wanted to ask him about you, but he was missing."

"Missing?" That bothered him more than the fact she'd gone to find out about himself.

She pulled her legs under her so she was kneeling. "Yes. I tried multiple times at his office, but he was nowhere to be found. Then when I tried to join you, I couldn't get any closer in time then when I arrived."

"I don't like it." Now they were being micromanaged, but not even by their own boss.

She shook her head. "I don't either. Now, I doubt every move we make."

At her continued use of the word "we," a warmth settled in his chest. They may not know exactly what was going on, but he liked that they were working as a team. Another vibration against his back reminded him it was time to leave. He rose and held his hand out to her. "I think we should get back to our charge."

Joy placed her hand in his, a shy smile on her face. "Thank you. I enjoyed our break."

He cupped her cheek in his other hand. "I did, too." He gave her a light kiss on the lips, not completely comfortable with the caring he saw in her eyes.

After their assignment, if they both still had jobs and if Cameron was still their boss, there was no guarantee they would see much of each other. That thought had his gut tightening. He didn't like that at all.

"Shall we?" Joy's brow rose with her question as she phased.

"Aye."

<h1 style="text-align:center">Chapter Nine</h1>

Joy held Malcolm's hand, pondering the new feelings she had as they flew toward Holly. Something had definitely changed in him, which put to rest her panicked reaction to his vigilante work. He must have not made any mistakes there or he wouldn't be in the afterlife. At least, she hoped that was the case.

They reappeared just as Holly's foot disappeared into the dining room of Sarah and Brody's home. Following their charge, they floated in behind her and listened to the couple's conversation. At least Sarah managed a smile now and then.

Malcolm let go of her hand to move in front of Holly. "Are you ready for your next visit?"

She nodded. "Who's leading the way?"

Malcolm chuckled. "I am."

"Really?" Holly looked to her. "You're going to let him break my heart twice in a row. There's so much sadness in my future, I don't know what to try to fix first."

Joy took hold of Holly's hand. "It's not about fixing things. It's about having meaningful relationships with others. If you do that, you won't have to 'fix' anything."

"I don't understand."

Malcolm took Holly's other hand. "Then allow me to show you." He pulled them up through the ceiling and into the gray ether.

When it cleared, they hovered above the same house. "We're here, but I need to explain these next two visits."

Holly looked at him. "But we didn't go anywhere."

"Actually, we did." Malcolm let her go and faced her. "What you will see next is a future you."

"A future me? Is there more than one?"

He smiled. "Aye. This future has a forty percent chance of happening."

Holly grimaced. "That's not very good odds."

Joy chuckled. "Because you're still with us, those are the best odds there are. They can change based on your decisions. After you see this future you, I'll show you the other one that has an equal chance of coming true."

"Then I get to choose which path I want to take, right?" Holly's eyes lit with excitement.

"Correct." Malcolm opened his arm toward the roof top. "Are you ready?"

"Yes." Holly let go of Joy's hand and sped through the roof.

Quickly, they followed into the now Christmas decorated living room.

Holly pointed at her future self, sitting on an ottoman next to a baby lying on a blanket on the floor. "Well, at least I look pretty healthy. I was almost afraid I'd become a leper or something." She chuckled, missing the look Malcolm threw her way.

"Oh, and look at that little thing. Tell me that's Sarah's." Holly looked at Malcolm who nodded.

"What a cutie." Holly floated closer as the baby rolled onto her tummy and tried to move forward.

"She's not getting into anything, is she?" Sarah called from the other room.

The older Holly smiled. "Now what could she possibly get into? She's barely scooting yet." She looked at the clock to the right of the fireplace where a large picture of Sarah, Brody, Holly, Cameron and Ethan hung. "I think the men got lost at the Black Raven Pub on their way back."

Sarah laughed. "They better not have or they'll have to watch the children tomorrow. That's the deal."

"Mummy?" The two-year-old voice could be heard in the other room.

Holly floated to the doorway before looking back at them. "How wonderful! They have two children." She smiled as a little boy came to the door.

"Mummy?" The little boy with brown wavy hair grabbed a hold of the doorframe with one hand. In his other hand was a half-eaten cookie. "Cookie?" He held it out toward the older Holly.

"Is that for me, honey?" The Holly on the ottoman opened her arms.

The little boy broke into a big smile as he toddled toward his mom.

Joy watched the younger Holly's face go white, her eyes round with shock. "How can this be?" She continued to watch as the older Holly picked up the little boy and made a production of eating the cookie he gave her.

Holly drifted back to them, avoiding the pair on the ottoman as if they were diseased. "Why are you showing me this?"

Joy wanted to give Holly a hug, but refrained.

Malcolm's voice was low and soft. "Because this is a future you could have."

Holly shook her head. "I can't. How can I? I love Cameron and he's gone." Her voice cracked on her last word, though she couldn't take her eyes off her future self, her eyes still round with shock.

"You have the capacity to love many people."

Holly's gaze flew to Malcolm's at his words. "You want me to love another man?" Her voice squeaked to a near panicked pitch.

Malcolm gave her a kind smile. "*I* don't want you to do anything. I'm merely showing you what possible future you can have." He reached out his hand toward the little boy. "You could even have a son to love."

She shook her head, her eyes filling with tears. "No." Before either of them could react, Holly had flown straight through the ceiling.

Joy threw Malcolm a worried look before following. When she reached the outside of the roof, Holly was nowhere to be seen. Oh sugar. This wasn't good.

Malcolm floated up beside her. "Where is she?"

"I don't know." Her stomach tightened. One of the few rules they had as spirit guides was to never, ever lose a living client, never mind Cameron's wife.

"We'll find her. Come. If we don't see her, we'll just go back in time." He grabbed her hand and floated them above the town. "There. She just phased into her old house." He pointed to the one-story house on Main Street.

She cringed. "That's not good either." They flew through time instead of space to be sure to catch Holly. When they phased into the house, Holly hovered in the middle of her living room with a scowl on her face.

Her attention snapped to them. "Who changed my house around?"

Joy moved forward, her heart still beating a little too fast from her scare. "In this future, you don't live here anymore."

Holly's scowl deepened. "Who lives here?" She scanned the room frantically, her confusion palpable, her worry obvious.

Malcolm answered. "Brooke lives here. She manages the shop for you."

At that, Holly's body seemed to lose all its tension. "I still own the One of a Kind Christmas Shop?" The relief in her eyes was heartbreaking.

Joy couldn't resist any longer. She knew better than to get too emotionally close to a client, but Holly needed a hug. She wrapped her arms around her. "Yes. You still own the shop, it's still called that, and you still offer only one-of-a-kind Christmas decorations."

Holly nodded against her shoulder. "Good."

She pushed the woman back. "I'm sorry this happy visit wasn't so happy for you."

"No, it wasn't. I should have known because Malcolm brought me there." She gave him a scowl as if he'd caused it.

Joy couldn't let that pass. "No, it wasn't Malcolm's fault. What you saw was caused by your own decisions."

Holly shook her head. "I can't believe that."

"Would you like to see how else your life could be in the same time period?"

"Yes. You said it was only a forty percent chance for either, right?"

"That's true. There's also a twenty percent chance that your future will be something completely different. It will all depend on the choices you make after tonight."

Holly wiped her wet cheeks with the sleeve of her sweater. "Let me see what my other most probable choice led to."

Joy nodded and took her hand. As she reached for Malcolm's hand, she found him deep in thought. "Are you ready?"

He jerked to attention before clasping her hand. "Aye."

She floated them through the wall into the shop next door. It was open, but no customers filled the space. There weren't as many decorations and the ones that were there were full of dust.

At the front counter sat Holly. She wore no Santa cap and her black sweater had no Christmas design. She stared out the front window, a frown on her face as people bustled past.

"I don't look so good." Holly moved closer to her older self, before glancing around the shop. "Where is everyone?"

"You don't get many customers anymore."

"Of course not. Look at the dust on everything. Most of this inventory I recognize from this year. It should have sold by now. What happened?" She floated by, inspecting the shelves before stopping at the fifteen-foot Christmas tree. "This is unacceptable." She scowled at a pinecone ornament whose glitter was so coated in dust, it didn't shine at all.

Joy joined her. "No one wants to shop here anymore. You get the occasional tourist, but all your local customers avoid it."

Holly snorted. "I can see why. What I want to know is why did I let it get so run down?"

Joy couldn't think of a nice way to explain, so she took a page from Malcolm's playbook. After all, Cameron said not to be subtle. "Because you have no life. People still like you, but you have no substance. You attend events and chat as you shop. But you don't have any close relationships and the ones you had, you didn't keep up. You don't do anything new."

Holly crossed her arms. "Are you saying I'm not fun to be around?"

Malcolm came over to stand next to Joy. "No, you smile at the right times and engage in conversation. You do make a suggestion on occasion, but your life is only what you know of others. You in particular don't do anything besides visit and work here."

"But I do still have the shop?" The hope in Holly's eyes was frustrating to see.

Joy looked at Malcolm and he nodded for her to answer. "Not for long. The only reason it's still here is because you sold the house next door to keep it open. You sleep in the office."

"What?" Holly flew across the room and disappeared behind a closed door.

Joy's stomach tightened. "Should I follow her?" Holly's disappearance at the last visit still had her rattled.

Malcolm shook his head. "I think she'll return shortly.

He was right. Holly floated out to them, her eyes already filling with tears. "I can't believe I sold Cam's and my home for this place."

"You had a choice to make." Malcolm's voice wasn't as hard as it had been on the other visits. "You couldn't keep both. And when your mom and John offered to help, you wouldn't hear of it. Probably because except for an occasional phone call, you didn't have a relationship with them anymore either."

Holly frowned, a tear finally falling on her cheek. "But why? I don't understand what happened."

Joy tried to think of a way to phrase it without pushing Holly toward one decision or the other. "It was a slow progression into not caring and a focused obsession. It's not any one single event exactly. It's simply what's the most probable outcome of you holding on to Cameron's memory as the priority of your life."

Holly threw her hands up. "In other words, I'm either supposed to forget Cam existed and marry someone else or keep our love alive and live a miserable existence." Holly's tears started to fall, but they were caused by a mix of hurt and anger and pure frustration. "That's my choice?"

"Except for the twenty percent probability that you beat the odds." She gave her a half-hearted smile.

As Holly squinted her eyes in anger, Malcolm stepped in. "None of this would even be shown to you if you hadn't been Cameron's wife. He's pulled strings to help you."

Holly snapped her gaze to him. "Wait a minute. I didn't ask him to come visit me two years ago. That was *his* choice."

Malcolm opened his mouth to answer, but Joy interrupted. "True, but who asked him to come back again and again?"

Once again, Holly crossed her arms. "I wouldn't have even known that was possible if he didn't visit me in the first place."

Malcolm pounced on that. "And he wouldn't need to visit you from the grave if he'd appreciated what you had to begin with."

Holly nodded before she stopped, her eyes wide. She shook her head and turned away. "This isn't Cam's fault. It was an accident."

Joy flew around her before Malcolm did. "But he knew the risks of rock climbing on such a cold day. He did leave you on Christmas day despite the icy conditions. He may not have known that he would fall, but he knew it was a possibility."

Holly stopped shaking her head. "I just wish we could go back in time and do that day over."

Malcolm joined them. "Even if you could, that wouldn't stop him from doing something else that was risky. If you could relive that day and change the outcome, there's a good chance you'd still lose him too soon."

"We don't know that." She looked away, desperately searching for an argument. "You said Brody stopped taking risks. Why not Cameron?"

Joy's heart squeezed. To see such a steadfast love and know her job was to break it apart was hard. "Because Brody's behavior only changed *after* Cameron's death. It took something that drastic."

Malcolm put his hand on Holly's shoulder. "The probability of Cameron dying within that year is well over ninety percent."

Holly's mouth dropped open and her eyes rounded.

Joy searched her knowledge but she couldn't see probabilities. She could only see a number of devastating events. Malcolm knew the probabilities because he was from the future. She wished she could see with that kind of clarity.

A sudden thought occurred to her. Would he know the probability of her niece having lived or died? That unknown kept niggling at her like sand in her shoe, interrupting her focus at inopportune times. She watched him study Holly. He might be her only chance to find out.

"You have to tell him." Holly grabbed Malcolm's arm. "You have to. He's riddled with guilt over that day. You have to tell him he was fated to die that year. Don't let him beat himself up anymore. It's not fair. Let him blame it on fate. Release him from his guilt, please!"

That's what this was all about? Cameron's guilt? Joy felt a mixture of relief and anger. So, she and Malcolm were pawns sent to accomplish what? To free Cameron of his guilt? Free Holly of her anger? That wasn't enough. Holly deserved her own happily ever after.

As for Cameron, Joy wasn't sure she cared at the moment.

"I'll tell him." Malcolm nodded, and Holly let go of him.

"Thank you. If he knows that, will he still visit me?" The hope in her watery eyes was frustrating.

"I don't know." Malcolm shrugged. "It's not up to him."

"Oh, that's right." Holly nodded, wiping the tears from her face. "He did say that he reported to someone else and this past year it was all about what I did. So maybe if I find that twenty percent probability path, I could see him again."

Joy's anger at Cameron got the better of her. Holly should be living her life for her, not for the chance to see her dead husband. "I'm not sure seeing him again is a good idea."

"Why not?" Holly turned to her in shock.

Making her decision, Joy spread her arms to encompass the quiet shop. "Because that's what causes this."

"But you said it was due to my—"

"Your choices. Yes, but you make those solely based on seeing Cameron again. I didn't want to say it, but I guess you need to know." Her blood was pumping hard. Releasing her calm and allowing her anger to dictate her actions as a spirit guide was new. "The decisions you make to see your dead husband, to live for him instead of yourself will all lead to your life being something like this."

Holly's mouth opened, but nothing came out. The mixture of pain and confusion in her eyes didn't bode well.

Malcolm took Joy's hand and gave it a squeeze.

She sincerely hoped that meant what she'd said was a good thing because it didn't look good at the moment.

"You have a lot to think about now." Malcolm addressed Holly. "Are you ready to go back to your time?"

"That's it?" Holly looked lost. "But there must be more you can show me."

Malcolm shrugged. "Like what? You don't have much of a life to show. Can you think of anything we might have missed? I can't."

Joy held her breath. Come on Holly. Think.

Holly frowned. "I have more of a life than this." She pointed to the shop then drifted to the window that looked out on Main Street.

They waited. Malcolm looked down at her, his face showing his disappointment. But they couldn't give up. If they did, it meant Holly would continue to waste her life.

Joy tried to think of something that would bring Ethan to mind. The fact that he was so far from Holly's was not a good sign.

Holly spun around. "What about Ethan? I'm worried about him and his future. Is everything okay with him? Did he ever tell the woman he was in love with that he loved her? What did she say? Can you at least tell me who it is so I can help him?"

Joy's heart felt a little lighter at Holly's outburst.

But Malcolm appeared unmoved. "What does Ethan have to do with you? You've avoided him for three years now."

"Oh no, don't you give me that. I've seen him at Brody and Sarah's and a few other events. Just because I'm not around him every week doesn't mean I don't care about how he's doing."

Joy didn't want to risk losing Holly's focus while she had it. "What do you think, Malcolm? Do you think she can handle Ethan's future?"

"I can." Holly nodded vigorously. "Who knows, maybe I can help him, and he can help me."

Malcolm smiled. "Maybe. I'm fine with visiting his future if Joy is."

"Please, Joy. I think it will help me get out of my own head."

She couldn't have resisted Holly's pleading brown eyes if she'd tried. She was thankful that Holly wanted this last visit. It just might sway her to being open to the possibilities of her future…without Cameron. "I think it will, too." She held out her hand. "Let's go."

Malcolm pulled up his hood and grasped Holly's other hand. Quickly, he led them through time, his own agenda not sitting well on his conscience. He wanted to take Joy into his confidence about their final step with Holly, but he couldn't risk her fighting him.

"I don't like this gray stuff."

Holly's complaint had him stifling a smile. "It will clear soon."

As soon as he said the words, the ether disappeared and they flew over a stately mansion on the outskirts of Deervale.

"Oh, that's Ethan's ancestral home." Holly pointed to the estate. "His parents live here."

"Not anymore." He floated them through the roof as he explained. "Ethan's parents moved into the house in town to be closer to their friends over a year ago. Didn't you know that?"

Holly looked away. "No, I didn't."

He brought them down just outside Ethan's study. "Why not? I thought you were interacting with your friends more."

She dropped his hand. "It's a little more complicated than that. I told you, Ethan is in love with someone, but I don't know who."

Joy let go of his hand and moved to stand in front of Holly. "Why not? Have you asked him?"

He liked this new straight-to-the-point Joy. She could almost be a Glasgow police woman.

Holly rolled her eyes at them. "It's not like I can come out and ask him. I'm not supposed to know, remember?" She turned away. "I've only seen him among other people, so it's hard to get into the kind of deep conversation I'd need to in order to dig into that."

Joy moved again to force Holly to look at her, something he would have done. "Didn't he ask you to have dinner at his parents' home in town? To go to the Deervale music festival? To have coffee the morning after Burns night?"

Holly looked away. "Obviously, you already know the answer to those questions."

"Yes, I do. What I don't know is why you didn't go. It was the perfect chance to discover who he loves." Joy's persistence pleased him. It was good to have a partner he could count on. *Then why aren't you telling her your plan to end this?*

Holly dropped her arms. "I didn't want to be alone with him, so if the woman he loves saw him, she wouldn't think he was with me."

Joy's face softened. "That was very thoughtful, but as you will see, it may have been the wrong choice."

Holly's gaze snapped to Joy's. "Ethan's okay, isn't he?"

Now was the time for him to push. Malcolm floated between the two women. "This is the future. You can decide for yourself." He opened his arm toward the study door.

Holly moved toward it, while Joy floated over to him, a small smile on her face. She leaned in and whispered. "Very Spirit of Christmas Future, Mr. Scrooge." Her gaze went from his arm to his hood.

He grinned back at her. "I try."

She gave a soft chuckle that sent sexual fission flashing up his spine.

Schitz. He wanted this assignment done so he could take her back to his cottage and make love to her for at least a week nonstop. Maybe longer? The implications of that knocked him off balance. He needed to look into exactly why he wanted Joy in his afterlife.

Joy found Holly floating above Ethan's desk, frowning at him.

"You look confused." She had to remember not to be subtle. Malcolm was so much better at this, but she was learning.

"Is Ethan drunk?"

She gave Holly a sad smile. "Yes."

Holly shook her head. "Why? Did the woman he loved reject him? Oh, poor Ethan. I need to be a better friend to him. Maybe if I do that, I can keep this from happening." Holly floated to where Joy was. "I can influence the future, right?"

Malcolm floated behind her, his bayberry scent letting her know where he was. He was close. His deep voice came over her left shoulder. "Aye, you can, but you have to remember, most of what you see tonight are scenes that are most likely to come true."

"But that's only if I don't change, right?"

Holly's hopeful look was hard to dismiss, but Joy ignored it. "That will only increase the probability that they won't come true." At Holly's crestfallen face, she forced herself to continue. "There's still a chance they will."

"This is so unfair to Ethan. He's such a good man. And look." Holly pointed at the man who sat at his desk in a t-shirt and gray sweats, his brown curly hair a mess, his green eyes blurry. The almost empty bottle of single-malt Scotch was next to his elbow, the glass in his hand, half empty. "He's handsome, too and well built."

Holly paused, her gaze running over Ethan's chest and arms. "Wow, he's really built. I never noticed that before. Probably because he's always in a collared shirt and a pair of trousers. He's smart. He manages his family's money. He went to the university with Cameron and Brody. He'd be a great catch for any woman. I'm so pissed a woman did this to him."

Joy glanced at Malcolm before addressing Holly. "Does Ethan rock climb like Cameron and Brody? He looks to be in good shape."

Holly shook her head. "Oh, no. He's the opposite of Cam and Brody. While they were impetuous and risk takers, Ethan always had to plan everything in advance and he was all about safety first. Sometimes it drove Cam crazy." Holly smiled at the memory.

"But this man." Malcolm opened his arm toward the drunk Ethan. "Tried to keep Cameron from going. He was the only one who took your side. He was the best kind of friend and now look at him."

Holly turned back to Ethan who was in the process of throwing back the rest of the Scotch. "Oh Ethan, I'm so sorry. I'll make this change. I swear."

Joy floated to Holly and took her hand to bring her away from Ethan. "It won't be that easy."

"Why not? All I have to do is reach out to him in my time."

"Watch."

The front doorbell rang, but Ethan just poured himself another shot.

The bell rang again.

Holly frowned. "Where's his mom? Or butler? Or whatever a place this big has?"

"As Malcolm said, Ethan's parents live in town now and he won't have any employees living with him. Everyone must go home by five so he can drink himself into oblivion." Joy stopped talking at the loud banging on the door.

"Well, someone obviously wants in pretty badly." Holly's observation was shared by Ethan since he stood, swayed, then staggered out of the study.

They all followed him.

It took him four tries, but eventually he managed to open the door.

Chapter Ten

"Ethan?" Sophia stared at Ethan as if she'd expected him to be drunk.

"Sophia? Why are you here?" He held on to the door for support.

At his words, Sophia broke into tears. "Oh, Ethan, I had nowhere else to go. No one else to talk to. You've always been so kind to me. I just needed some kindness right now."

He stared at her blankly. "I don't understand."

Sophia fell onto him, wrapping her arms around his neck, almost sending them both to the floor as she choked out her words. "My sister's dead. My poor little sister." Tears flowed over Sophia's cheeks.

Holly turned to them. "But you said if I befriended Sophia, her sister wouldn't die."

Joy shook her head. "No, we told you that you could befriend her and try to change the future. These scenes are simply the most probable given what has occurred up to your Christmas Eve this year."

"Then I'll just be sure this never happens. I knew Sophia had a heart under there somewhere. She doesn't deserve this. She may be a little self-involved, but—"

"She's very self-involved. Don't sugarcoat the truth just because her sister has died." Malcolm was obviously not going to be moved by Sophia.

"Fine." Holly gave him an irritated look. "Very self-involved, but she loves her sister. I'm going to do everything in my power to keep this from happening. I already told you that. What's next?"

Malcolm's jaw clenched and Joy cringed.

That didn't bode well. "There's more you still have to see. Come back into the study." She grabbed Holly's hand and Malcolm's and sped through time a few minutes.

Ethan now lay passed out on the couch in his study, his head resting on the arm, one leg on and one leg off. Sophia sat next to him. "Ethan? Are you awake?" When she didn't get a response, she smiled.

Holly looked at Joy, but she simply pointed at Sophia.

The woman rose from the couch and proceeded to undress, throwing her clothes about. Her blouse went on the desk, her bra on the end table near Ethan's head, her skirt was left on the floor along with a pair of thong panties. Lastly, she pulled off her high heels and placed one on the rug near the desk and the other on the end table nearest her.

Joy looked at Malcolm to see if he enjoyed the view, but he was looking at her. She flushed and quickly looked away.

Sophia bent over and carefully untied Ethan's sweatpants. She kept checking to make sure Ethan didn't wake up. Then slowly, she pulled Ethan's cock out.

Joy watched Holly's face. She stared, her mouth open, her eyes riveted. Her whole body shivered before she licked her lips.

"Holy crap!" Holly found her voice before looking at Joy then back to Ethan. "He's hung." Holly's gaze found Ethan's face again and softened. "He really is the whole package." Her voice held a sense of awe.

Joy hoped that meant Holly might be waking up, but she didn't want to count on it. She glanced down at the man's cock. It was thick and long and it wasn't even hard. In fact, it was a lot like Malcolm's. She swallowed.

"He's not going to be of any use to her passed out like that." Holly couldn't seem to stop staring at Ethan. That was definitely good.

Having set everything up, Sophia lay down on the couch next to the man, her head on his shoulder, her hand across his waist and one leg over his. She smiled as she closed her eyes.

Holly frowned. "I don't get it. She wants Ethan to think he slept with her? Is she that desperate for a boyfriend?" She turned to face them and her eyes grew round. "Oh, no. She's not going to accuse him of rape or anything is she?"

"No!" Joy couldn't let her think that. Sophia wasn't *that* bad.

Holly frowned. "Is she the one he's in love with. No, that can't be because he wouldn't love someone like her."

Joy pounced on that. "What kind of woman would Ethan love?"

"Someone kind, intelligent, helpful and who has bigger boobs than Sophia."

Joy laughed. Both she and Holly were well endowed compared to poor Sophia, whose figure was almost that of a teenage boy.

"I agree." Malcolm's comment had her growing self-conscious again.

Holly grinned. "It's nice to know you have such good taste in women." She looked between him and Joy.

Joy flushed. She prided herself on being professional. Could Holly tell they'd had sex?

"What's the deal with this?" Holly waved toward Sophia and Ethan on the couch. "Why would she do this? She's self-involved and Ethan is giving, so she's obviously going to take advantage of him. I have to stop this somehow."

Malcolm floated in front of them both and took their hands. At his touch, Joy felt like she was on fire. Watching Sophia and Ethan had her body remembering Malcolm's as they made love outside. This wasn't good. She needed to concentrate on this final visit.

Malcolm spun them around and they were looking at Ethan again, sitting at his desk. A full Scotch bottle was set on one side with an empty glass next to it, but it remained unopened.

Ethan wore a collared shirt, no tie and typed on his computer. His hair was as neat as it could be, considering its curly texture, and the light streaming in from the windows made it clear it was still during the day. A young man came in to announce Ethan had a visitor.

Holly floated toward Ethan. "This is the man I know. Have we gone back in time?"

Malcolm shook his head. "No, just a couple months forward."

Holly didn't seem to like that very much. Joy had a feeling the woman was anxious to find out more about Ethan's future. Little did she know there was plenty that would happen right now.

Ethan pushed his computer aside and rose as Sophia walked in, dressed in a pair of casual slacks and a sweater, but no coat, which made it clear it was probably fall.

"Sophia. This is a pleasant surprise." Despite his words, Ethan didn't return the hug she gave him. "What's the occasion? No, let me guess. You're checking on the foundation we set up in Thea's name."

Sophia shook her head and took a seat on the very couch she'd lain on with Ethan, and patted the spot next to her. "I need to talk to you."

Ethan didn't move to the couch. Instead, he leaned up against his desk opposite her, much like Cameron often did. Joy smiled at the thought. They may have been opposites, but there were some similarities.

Holly snorted. "If she's going to ask him for a favor, good

luck. I've seen that look on him before. He's not happy to see her. Whatever happened when he woke up to find her sprawled all over him certainly didn't make him sympathetic toward her."

Joy studied Ethan. "What look?"

Holly pointed to his right eyebrow. On the very edge toward his hairline there was a small tic.

"You must know him well. I would have never noticed that."

Holly grinned smugly. "Well, he was at our place more than his own when Cam was alive, especially after Brody met Sarah. I know almost as much about him as I do Cam. We were all inseparable."

"Then you avoiding him must be very difficult for him. Sounds like he was most comfortable around you all."

Holly looked back toward Ethan and frowned. "You're right. I did think about asking him to help me set up the Christmas tree this year, but that was always something Cam and I did together. I just couldn't."

Joy placed her hand on Holly's shoulder. "I know it's hard, but you need to be open to change. That is the only way you will be able to move on and embrace your future."

"I know, but it's hard. I really don't want to move on, yet you've shown me I have to for Cameron's sake."

Malcolm interceded. "For your sake, not Cameron's. It's the only way you'll be reunited in the afterlife."

"What? Cam didn't say that." At Holly's exclamation, Joy scowled at him. What was he trying to do?

Malcolm pointed at Holly. "That's because he's not allowed to, but I'll tell you, from everything I've observed so far, if you can't learn to live for you instead of your dead husband, there won't be a Cameron waiting for you."

Joy grabbed Malcolm's hand and pulled him out into the hall. "What are you doing?" Her words, meant to be a whisper came out in a hiss.

"I'm doing what needs to be done."

"You can't lie to her like that."

His face grew hard. "What makes you think I'm lying? Did you ever wonder why Cameron is sending spirit guides to Holly every year? If he was confident they would be together in the afterlife, why push her out of her grief? Could it really be just his own guilt, or is he being driven by a need to have forever with her?"

She didn't have an answer and her intuition told her he was on to something. "If that's the case, I'm not sure shocking her with that particular knowledge is the right strategy."

His lip quirked up on the right side. "Were you not the one who said we shouldn't be subtle?"

She pulled a stray strand of hair back behind her ear. "I understand that, but we've given her so many shocks already. I'm worried about how much more she can take."

"Shocking a living person into a new direction has worked every time for me."

Her stomach clenched at his words. "But that's why you are on this assignment in the first place. Remember, if you don't change your ways, you could disappear. I've become less subtle. Maybe you could be less shocking?"

He shook his head. "I don't think I'm supposed to change. I believe Cameron was told to tell me that so it would be harder to motivate Holly. I think he's the one on trial here, not me." The smile he gave her concerned her.

"But what if you're wrong? There has to be a middle ground you could take, just in case."

He gazed into her eyes, his brown ones revealing nothing of his thoughts. "Why do you care so much?"

Sugar, she'd walked in to that one. If there was any kind of caring in his gaze, she could admit the growing feeling in her chest, but there was nothing. Only the interrogator studying her like a suspect. Breaking his gaze, she shrugged. "Because I want us to be successful."

"Do you mean something like how you care for the families of your hospice patients."

Relieved at his assumption, she gave him a soft smile. "Yes, something like that."

His lip curled up into a sneer before he turned. At least she thought that's what it was. Quickly, she floated next to him. "Did I say something you don't like?"

He brushed it off. "No. Let's get back inside before Holly is overwhelmed by Sophia's scheming."

She nodded, but her stomach tied itself into knots. The last thing she wanted to do was hurt him, but there was no way she could tell him that her feelings for him were evolving. She didn't have time to sort them out yet. All she knew was her concern arose from far more than attraction…and far more than for the families of her patients.

Malcolm grinded his teeth as they floated back into the study. He wasn't even entirely sure why he felt so frustrated, but he did. Why would Joy have a picture of him in her nightstand drawer before they'd even started this assignment if she only thought of him like a family member of a patient, a far more distant relationship than the photo indicated? He prided himself on reading his suspects, knowing if they would make a run for it or stay and face the consequences.

But she's not a suspect. You're not objective and she's your lover. His conscience just irritated him more. Aye, he'd hoped for something different in her answer. He'd thought he'd seen something in her eyes, but he must have been wrong.

It made the end to the assignment that much easier.

Sophia's voice interrupted his thoughts as he stopped next to

Joy. "I didn't expect to get pregnant, Ethan. I promise you. I just needed some comfort, and you needed some, too."

Ethan rubbed the back of his neck, obviously unhappy.

Holly floated next to the man. "Don't do it, Ethan. It's a trick. She must have become worse after Thea died. Don't give in."

"Sophia, I'm half to blame and I'll be a part of this baby's life. It's the right thing to do."

"No, Ethan, don't." Holly's upset gave Malcolm something to work with.

"Thank you. I always knew you were a good man." Sophia rose and kissed Ethan on the cheek. "I'll come back on the weekend with my things. In such a large house, you'll hardly know I'm here."

Holly turned to Joy, tears in her eyes. "There has to be some way to stop this. Tell me, if I can keep Thea from dying, will this *not* happen?"

Before Joy could open her mouth, he spoke. "Only one thing can stop this from happening."

Holly's face snapped to him. "What?"

"If the woman he loved, loved him back."

"But I don't know who that is!" A tear slipped down her cheek, and Joy took her hand.

She could give all the comfort she wanted to Holly, but he would make the woman open her eyes. "Pay attention and you'll figure it out."

At his words, Holly's face lit with a tremulous smile. "I will."

While they spoke, Sophia had exited the room. Malcolm felt a certain sympathy with Ethan. The man had just been duped by a woman much like he'd been duped by his "wife," Coira. At least Ethan wouldn't pay with his life like he had.

But as Ethan reached for the Scotch bottle and poured a shot of whiskey into the empty glass, Malcolm had his doubts about the longevity of Ethan's life.

Holly watched Ethan much like he'd seen Joy looking at himself, with sympathy. Sympathy was worthless. Action was what was needed.

Ethan walked around to the other side of his desk and picked up his phone. "Call Mum." As he waited, Holly wiped her tears with the back of her hand.

"Hi Mum. Aye, I'll be there Sunday. No nothing's wrong, well, except I wanted to let you know that Sophia Dunlap is going to be staying in the east wing for a bit."

Holly shook her head, a scowl on her face. Malcolm had no sympathy for her. A lot of this was her fault.

Ethan continued. "I know, but she came to me and you're the one who taught me to never turn away from a friend."

Malcolm pointedly looked at Holly, and she flushed. Good.

Ethan sat in his chair and sighed. "I don't think it would make much difference to tell her I love her. She seems to have forgotten we were once friends." Ethan gave a pathetic chuckle. "No Mum, it's not an American thing. She doesn't even know I exist anymore."

Malcolm watched Holly closely. She was intent on Ethan's conversation, but there was no recognition in her face.

Ethan looked up at the ceiling as if finding his patience. "No, I won't do that. Did you want me to bring Sophia with me on Sunday?"

Holly whispered as if Ethan could overhear. "He didn't say anything about a baby. Do you think he's skeptical?"

Malcolm opened his mouth, but Joy stepped in. "I'm sure he is since he doesn't remember that night."

Ethan reached for the glass of Scotch with his free hand. "Right, I'll pick him up on my way over. See you then." With one hand, he ended the conversation and with the other, he threw back the shot of whiskey.

Holly frowned, floating closer to Ethan. "I'm so sorry. I did this." She waved her hand at the whole room. "I did all of this."

Joy drifted forward as if she'd offer comfort. "You didn't know. How could you?"

Holly glanced at him. "I could have if I'd been a good friend like he'd been to me."

He nodded.

Joy glanced back at him before facing Holly again. "You were grieving. You needed some time. You just took too long."

"You're right. This is all wrong. I can change this."

"How?" Malcolm pulled Holly's attention from Joy. "How will you fix this?"

"Tomorrow. He invited me to his parents for Christmas day. I'll go. If he needs someone to talk to about Cameron, I'll be there for him."

He pressed his advantage. "But that's not all he needs from you."

Joy gave him a nervous look, but Holly kept shaking her head, now having a dose of her own guilt. "This isn't right. How could anyone be his friend and forget he exists. Is it someone from when he attended the university?"

Malcolm felt like Ethan wasn't the only one who had lost patience. "No. Think. What woman do you know who used to be friends with Ethan and is American?"

Holly's brow lowered as she thought. "I didn't know he knew any Americans but me." She stared at him, and he raised his eyebrows.

"Oh no." She shook her head. "You don't mean…he loves… but I didn't know…how can—" She closed her mouth, her eyes wide.

Joy moved in like Florence Nightingale. "Of course you didn't." She looked at him with disbelief.

He ignored her. "But think of all your actions for the last three years from his point of view, and this is even farther into the future. The woman he loves pushes him away every time. Do you wonder he drinks himself into a stupor every night?"

"That's it." Joy grabbed his arm. "You overstepped."

He refused to be moved. "He's loved you for a long time. After Cameron's death, he thought it was just a shared sympathy, his heart aching for you in your grief. Then he realized it was something more. He's wanted to tell you but out of respect didn't push you…for three long years. Then, as you see, he gave up. You made that easy since you avoid him."

Holly shook her head. "But I can't."

He floated toward Holly, but Joy blocked his way. "I think you've done enough."

He stared at her. His anger at Holly didn't make sense. He was law enforcement. He kept his cool, his objectivity. Why be angry at—he was angry at the wrong woman. "Cameron Douglas, come here!"

Joy's eyes grew round. "What are you doing? You can't call him here."

He lifted his head to shout toward the ceiling. "Cameron Douglas, your wife needs help!"

Joy grabbed him as if she could stop him from shouting. "Malcolm, don't. Please."

He stared into her eyes which were filled fear. "Why not?"

"I'm afraid for you."

He grabbed her shoulders. "Why?"

She looked away.

He'd seen something there. He had to know why.

"What's going on?" Cameron Douglas floated through the ceiling and directly toward Holly. "Hen, are you okay?"

She shook her head.

He threw them a look of rage before he gathered his wife into his arms.

At his boss's contact with his wife, a small doubt crept into Malcolm's conscience. Could the man keep his time with her limited, or had he just sentenced Cameron to a ghostly existence?

He pushed the thought away. If he was right, this was Cameron's test and he had his own woman to deal with. Without a word, he let go of her shoulders, grabbed her hand and swept them into the ether.

Joy tried to pull away. "We can't leave. We have to fix this with Cameron."

Her struggles were fierce, but he was far stronger. The ether cleared as he landed them in his living room and he let her go.

She spun on him, her eyes filled with unshed tears. "We need to go back. Don't you understand? Cameron will dismiss you and you'll never be seen again."

His heart lurched. "Why do you care if that happens?"

"Because I don't want you to disappear. Don't you understand?"

His chest tightened as emotion threatened to choke off his words. He lowered his voice. "Joy, why don't you want me to disappear."

She pushed a stray strand of hair back behind her ear. "I care about you."

He forced himself not to cross the room and take her in his arms. "Why?"

At that, she rolled her eyes. "You can't figure that out?"

He shook his head. He needed to hear it.

"I care because you're kind and honorable and caring and smart and…" she shrugged.

"And what?" She made him sound like a paragon of virtue which he wasn't, but he needed to hear everything.

A tremulous smile formed on her lips. "And you're sexy squared to the tenth power."

His ego swelled at her words, but it wasn't what he wanted to hear. He finally moved toward her.

She backed up a step, and he grasped her arm. Her eyes widened as she looked up at him. Did he appear that scary?

He lifted his other hand to cup her face and an electric shock had them both jumping apart.

"Will you fuxing let me touch the woman I love? What is wrong with you?"

Joy stared at him in shock.

He loved her. A warmth settled around his heart as if all the cracks and gouges filled in. He felt whole.

A movement in the window behind Joy caught his attention. The green colored mist swirled to form two golden eyes and whiskers. The eyes squinted as if laughing before the image disintegrated. What in the afterlife was that?

"Malcolm?" Joy's voice brought his attention back to her. Her turbulent turquoise eyes glowed with a new warmth. "You love me?"

"Aye, I do." He'd tried to resist, but he'd been helpless against her sweet happy soul. She was an unexpected delight on so many levels.

When she didn't say anything, his heart started to ramp up. "I'm hoping maybe ye feel a wee bit for me as well."

"Oh yes!" She stepped forward then halted. "I do love you and I want to touch you." Her brow lowered in worry.

He glanced at the window behind her. Did that mean they'd never be able touch each other in his cottage? Was he supposed to keep his future sexual methods away from her? If that was the case, he'd gladly do it to be with her.

He stepped closer to her. "I want to touch you, too. Take my hand."

Gingerly, she clasped his hand.

As much as he wanted to pull her against him, he couldn't risk the pain to her. "Now you touch my arm."

"Maybe we should go outside."

He grinned because that's exactly where he was headed if that was their only option, but he needed to be sure. "Just use your finger."

Hesitantly, she held out her hand. As her finger hovered over his wrist, he held his breath. Finally, her light touch was on his skin. Her gaze snapped to his. "I don't understand."

Afraid to hope, he kept his excitement to himself. "Now use your whole hand."

She grasped his wrist. Still, there was no shock.

He smiled, gazing at her with all that he felt. He raised his hand still clasped by hers and cupped her cheek. "It's okay now."

"Why?"

He shrugged. "I think a certain entity didn't want me to have you here unless it meant more than simply sex."

Joy's eyes glittered with mischief. "I would have been okay with that."

He laughed, the action freeing. "I know and so would I, but I think we were meant to fall in love."

"You really do love me?"

"Ach, lass, from the moment I saw beneath your poised exterior, I started falling for you."

She cocked her head and looked up at him through her lashes. "And when was that?"

"When I discovered you had a piercing." He'd explain exactly when that was later.

She winked. "If I'd known that was all it took, I would have told you about it the second time we passed each other in the spirit lounge."

"That soon?"

She nodded. "Oh yes. I've been half in love with you since the first time we met. I was so afraid you'd find out and laugh at me."

He pulled her into his embrace. "I could never laugh at you. You fill the dark, empty places in my soul and make me want happiness again."

"Oh, Malcolm." At the look of love in her eyes, he lowered

his lips to hers and gave her the kind of kiss only a consummate deserved.

When he pulled away, her eyes were shining once again with unshed tears. "What is it? What's wrong?"

She shook her head. "Nothing. I'm just so happy."

He gave her a seductive smile. "I can make you even happier if you'd like."

She wrapped her arms around his neck. "Oh, I'd like."

Laughing, he scooped her up into his arms and headed for his bedroom, anxious to show her how much he could worship her both body and soul.

Chapter Eleven

Joy thought her heart would jump out of her body it was so full of happiness. Never had she imagined Malcolm would love her. He was darkness and strength and she was light and soft, but it had happened. And in the afterlife, no less.

She was still adjusting to her dreams coming true when Malcolm gently laid her on his bed. She could barely see anything as the room was dark. In fact, it didn't seem to have any windows.

He stepped away. "Open ceiling." At his words, the ceiling rolled back to reveal a series of square windows that looked into the green mist between his mountains. From where she lay, she could see the peak of one. It bathed the room in a beautiful green light. It was beaut—she swallowed as she leaned up on her elbows.

Malcolm's bedroom was a tribute to everything sensual. On the walls, painted directly into the stucco, were murals depicting various sexual acts between men and women, two women, two men, threesomes, foursomes, and even orgies.

The sex itself ranged from simple, to toys she'd never seen before, contraptions she was sure didn't exist in her time, to bondage. One scene in particular caught her attention. A man with a pierced cock and a woman with pierced nipples were being led by a man who held chains attached to their piercings.

"Do you see anything you like?" Malcolm's voice had changed. Here was the sexual man she'd sensed when he'd walked by her in the lounge.

She moved her gaze across the various images, well aware that already her body was excited. "Maybe. There are some I'm not sure what is happening."

His lip quirked up. "Allow me to educate you." He gestured to one wall. "Motion, no sound."

The painted figures started to move as if a porn movie played inside the wall itself except without live people. She stared as one woman straddled a man on what looked to be a weight bench only the head was lower than the hips. Another man pushed her forward and dribbling lube down her ass then proceeded to thrust inside her butt hole while she continued to ride the man beneath her.

Joy tried to close her mouth, but she seemed to need it to bring in more air as her gaze fell on a woman attached to a wall with furry manacles. Another woman lifted a bucket and poured what looked like a red syrup all over the other woman. Within seconds it had dried on her like a candy apple. Two men joined the syrup woman and began to eat away at the woman against the wall, who was obviously enjoying every moment.

Joy swallowed. "I knew I wasn't *that* experienced, but this is far more than I imagined." She looked sideways at one woman who had brought out something that looked like a whip, but seemed to have a mind of its own as it curled around a man's cock. "And I'm pretty sure there are a number of these I have no interest in."

Malcolm smiled. "I'm glad to hear that."

Her body relaxed. She'd been afraid that he was into *every* act. At least half held no interest to her, while others… She watched a man pull a string from inside a woman's sheath then eat the large nugget that popped out, only to pull on the string again until another treat was revealed. That both the treat and the woman's clit were devoured by his mouth had Joy's own sheath moistening. "These aren't depictions of real acts, are they?"

He nodded. "Oh, they are. In fact, this was one of the most sought-after reels of my time."

"Reels?"

"Yes, that's what these were called. Painted sexual scenes that come to life." He strode around his bed to the other wall. "This is what I'd like to do to you now."

She studied the act in progress. A naked man with black hair dribbled oil on a woman lying on her stomach on a cushioned table. "A massage?"

He grinned. "With a bonus."

"That sounds wonderful." Suddenly, she stilled. "But what about Holly?"

"Massage table." At Malcolm's command, a table rose up from the floor. "Holly couldn't be in better hands right now. We need to let the two of them figure things out. I'm sure Cameron will find us when he wants to."

He was right. Holly was in good hands, but she still worried about Malcolm. They needed to make sure that he could keep his job and based on Cameron's reaction, that didn't seem likely. *Don't be subtle.* Of course! Cameron had basically told them what to do. Maybe he wanted to be Holly's knight in shining armor.

"Joy?" Malcolm, completely naked, stood next to the bed, holding out his hand.

She smiled and put her hand in his.

"Turn around so I can get you out of your clothes."

"I can simply—"

"I know, but I want to undress you for a change." His eyes seemed to shine with a warm glow that had her body shivering in response.

She turned around, and he unzipped her green velvet dress,

slipping it off her shoulders, down her arms to puddle at her feet. He crouched, holding the dress as she stepped from it.

Malcolm threw it over a strange looking chair before turning back to look at her. "If I'd known what sexy under things you wear, I would have undressed you slowly before now."

She laughed. "No, you wouldn't have. You were too anxious to get me naked."

"And get inside you." At his words, her breath hitched.

"Turn around slowly. I want to see you." He motioned with his hand what he wanted.

She was happy to comply. She wore a soft white corset with thigh highs attached by dainty flowered garters. Beneath it was a thong of pale green lace. She slowly turned, allowing him to look all he wanted. When she finally faced him, his cock was hard and proudly sticking out.

A secretive smile curled his lips. "Beautiful."

It wasn't the word, but how he said it that caused her to flush.

Before she could respond, he knelt at her feet. "I love these old-fashioned garters." His large fingers nimbly worked the hooks on the front and back of her thigh. Then he purposefully rolled the nylon down to her boot. Lifting her foot as if he were Cinderella's prince, he removed her boot and rolled the nylon completely off.

Again, he rose and put her thigh high by the odd chair before returning to undress her other leg. When he'd completed that one, he returned and turned her around. Deftly, he unhooked the back of her corset, pulling it from her torso. As he put that away, she remained where she was.

She felt him stand against her back, his hands coming around to cup her breasts. "I'm going to make you come three times before you stand on your feet again." His voice brushed by her ear, causing her to shiver, though it could well be his words that caused that.

One hand moved from her breast to grasp the front of her

thong, and she held her breath. The other hand moved over her shoulder to glide down her back.

"Are you wet for me?" His whispered words caused more moisture to fill her folds.

She nodded.

"Good." His hand at her back grasped the top of her thong and slowly pulled upward, tightening the lacy string between her ass cheeks, sensitizing her anal hole and smearing her wetness. "Not that I don't believe you. I just want to see it."

He continued to pull until the panties were pressing her barbell in her clit hood and she jerked at the spike of excitement.

As if it was exactly what he'd waited for, he lowered the thong down to her feet and took it off.

"Ach, definitely a good start."

She turned around to see him add the thong to her pile of clothes. Then he took her hand and led her to the cushioned table. The top almost looked like it was made of twenty separate square cushions.

When Malcolm moved to the side and dropped four of them, leaving two holes big enough for her breasts, her curiosity rose. "Why do I have the feeling this is no ordinary massage table."

He kicked out a step and pulled her toward it. "Because it's not. It's made for sex."

She could always count on him to be straight forward. She lay down, fitting her boobs into the holes which made it so much more comfortable. Malcolm then took two more squares out so she could look down.

He hit a lever and a mirror slid out below her, giving her a perfect view of the figures moving on the wall. It was strange to be so excited when a massage was supposed to relax.

Malcolm's footsteps were barely audible on the stone floor, but when he stepped on the step behind her, she knew he was ready to begin.

"Sex oil." No sooner had he called for it than she felt the warm liquid dribble down her back and over her ass. There must have been a lot of advancements in sex play since her time because she'd never seen such a table and some of the toys on the reel were completely foreign to her.

Preferring to enjoy Malcolm as opposed to the wall scenes, she closed her eyes the moment his large hands ran over her back. He moved methodically, kneading her muscles with his hands, gentle yet strong. The scent of peppermint made her smile. He knew her so well.

It didn't take long for every one of her limbs to feel like jelly in the summer sun. He worked from her shoulders to her finger tips. From her ass to the bottoms of her feet and everywhere in between.

She felt his weight as his hands came on both sides of her, and he whispered in her ear. "Are you comfortable?"

She didn't even want to move her mouth, so she hummed, "Uh-huh."

His soft chuckle skittered over her skin, but didn't penetrate her stupor. He spread her legs apart and she heard a couple more squares drop away, but other than that, she hovered between wakefulness and sleep.

Malcolm's hands moved up the inside of her legs now, massaging her already lax muscles, but as he came closer to the juncture of her thighs, her skin started to wake. His hands moved over her ass and up her back again missing her wanting parts.

She heard a soft buzz and when his right hand touched her back, it vibrated as it massaged. It had her muscles tingling in their limp state. His vibrating hand moved over her ass and down her legs as she struggled to stay awake.

Then Malcolm stepped back, and she opened her eyes to find him adjusting the mirror below her so it showed her breasts. His hand with a band around his wrist came up and vibrated against her relaxed nipples, bringing them to life even though the rest of her was curiously limp.

He grinned into the mirror. "Just setting you up for what's to come." As soon as he teased her with his words, he unhooked two clips on chains from the sides of the table and attached them onto her hard nubs. Fire flew from her nipples to her core, which tensed with desire.

"Just one more adjustment."

She watched as he flicked a switch, but it was three seconds before the first buzz hit her left nipple. "Oh." The vibration surprised her, but then subsided, only to repeat the feeling on her right nipple, but for longer this time.

Malcom winked at her in the mirror. "Enjoy the show."

When he'd moved out of the way, she saw that the clips on her nubs glowed different colors depending on the type of vibration and there was no specific pattern. Though her muscles couldn't tense at the scattered stimuli, her folds filled with her readiness.

Suddenly, more oil hit just her butt, the scent slightly different, yet still minty. As Malcolm massaged it over her ass, spreading her cheeks and allowing it to completely cover her, she felt those areas tingle. Then his vibrating hand followed suit, stroking down her crease, tantalizing her anal hole, parts of her body waking up, but if he asked her to move on her own, she didn't think she could.

When that same hand touched her mons, she realized the gap the missing blocks had made. Her belly rested securely on the cushioned table, but Malcolm stood between her knees now.

She barely registered that fact before the hand vibrations traveled over her clit and opening, hitting her barbell and sending a jolt of excitement to her core, just as both nipple clips squeezed her quickly. She sucked in her breath, her insides coming alive while her muscles remained in complete lethargy. It was an odd sensation of helplessness and desire.

Malcolm's hand didn't simply vibrate as a whole, but each finger did as well, and as he slipped one inside her wet sheath, her heartbeat picked up. His other hand continued to massage her back as if he purposefully sent her body mixed signals.

He slipped his vibrating finger out and inserted another. It reminded her of her toys next to her bed. This was a feeling she knew well. When his thumb touched her barbell though, shocking pleasure sped up to her heart and through her opening, tightening her sheath around his fingers.

"You were made for this, for me." His words sent a feeling of rightness into her brain.

At the touch of his cock against her entrance at the same time the nipple clamps turned her hard nubs, her inner muscles tensed but the rest of her was still not willing to wake up. It was a titillating feeling. She could do little to direct her own pleasure. She'd have to depend on him.

Malcolm placed one hand on her back as he guided his cock inside her with his vibrating hand. "Perfect." His word was low and guttural, sending another spike of excitement deep inside her.

She could feel the vibration in her sheath until he let go. She expected him to pull out and thrust again, but he didn't. Instead, more warm tingling oil dripped onto her ass. He spread her cheeks and ran a vibrating finger down her crease, causing another spike of pleasure through her sheath and around his cock.

He sucked in his breath before bending over her. "Are you comfortable?"

She wanted to laugh but that would take too many muscles. "Very."

He squeezed her shoulder with his bare hand before running it down her back to her crease. He didn't stop there. When he came to her anal hole, he pressed against it with his finger.

The sexual excitement that sped to her core surprised her. She'd used a butt plug before, but Malcolm's finger was different. Slowly, he pushed his finger inside, inching it in, spreading her while her sheath's tension around his cock increased. Then the nipple clamps vibrated together, adding her to building need. She moaned.

"Now it's time to play." Malcolm's words sent a shiver down her back which he must have seen because he chuckled before his vibrating hand moved under his cock and his fist contacted her barbell.

Every nerve-ending inside her jumped, but she couldn't even lift her head. As lightning raced through her body, Malcolm began to move both his cock and finger out then in again, stimulating pleasure spikes. But with no muscle strength, she lay there, beyond excited but too limp to do anything except accept the double penetration, the vibrations on her clit and the random tweaks to her nipples.

She panted with desire, wanting to lift her hips to slam back against him as his cock slid inside to the hilt and his finger delved deep again. But she was helpless, her ecstasy creeping closer, forcing her to wait as her internal tension grew.

Finally, Malcolm's thrusts grew more forceful and rapid, causing her pleasure to spiral faster, her body rubbing forward against the cushioned table with every thrust before falling back into place as he pulled out.

She had no control over it at all, her entire feeling concentrated in the small region between her legs and ass until her orgasm finally hit. She saw stars as ecstasy blasted through her, starting between her thighs and sending jolts of euphoria slicing through her body. Malcolm's come filled her, making her bliss complete.

Her inability to yell seemed to make it last longer, her limp body vibrating with the impact of such a powerful orgasm for minutes upon minutes. She felt Malcolm's hands leave her body, which helped her breathing considerably.

He bent over, reaching his hand around to release the clamps before kissing her temple. "Did you enjoy?"

She licked her dry lips. "Very much."

He stood again and slowly pulled out of her.

She moaned at the loss, but felt even more like a rag doll than before.

He chuckled. "I'm thinking we need to rejuvenate you a bit."

She thought that was an excellent idea, but was far too tired to comment.

"Hot tub."

At Malcolm's words, she popped her eyes open and in the reflection of the mirror below her saw steam rising.

Malcolm's face interrupted her view. "Ready?" His lip quirked up in amusement.

She'd love to wipe the smug look off his face, but she was far too content to do anything about it. "Whenever you are."

He chuckled before disappearing from view.

The next moment she was phased, floated into the tub and solidified in his arms. She sighed. There was no place she'd rather be.

~~*~~

Holly felt Cameron's arms around her and her heart sighed. His distinctive clove scent filled her nostrils and his hard body kept her safe like it used to.

"You're far too enticing while phased like myself." He pushed her back, shaking his head. "Let me take you home."

Her heart ached at his rejection, though she knew in her mind he feared becoming a ghost because they had such a strong connection. Still, it hurt.

He didn't look at her, but grabbed her hand and brought them into the gray ether she didn't like. Luckily, it was a short trip.

As soon as they landed in their overly-decorated living room, he solidified her, making it impossible for them to touch again. That just hurt more. Tired of being taken through an emotional rollercoaster, she needed answers. "Cam, did you know Ethan was in love with me?"

"Not at first."

She raised her brows. "When?"

He didn't look at her when he answered. "After Coco and Ian visited you."

She crossed her arms as that betrayal was added to her heart. "She knew and didn't tell me?"

"Yes. I think she wanted to tell you, but Ian didn't think you were ready."

"How could I ever be ready with that news?" She threw her hands up. "At least if they had told me, I wouldn't have been such a bad friend this last year."

He snapped his gaze to hers at that. "What would you have done?"

Knowing he loved me? What could she do? It wasn't like she could love him back. The image of Ethan sprawled on his couch flitted through her mind, causing her heart to squeeze.

She pushed the picture away. She was Cameron's wife. "I don't know what I would have done, but at least I wouldn't have avoided him and caused what I did. Do you know Sophia Dunlap is going to trick him into believing he's the father of a baby by her?"

He nodded. "I knew it was a possibility. Only spirits from the actual future can give probabilities. The rest just see many alternative scenarios and use the ones that will help the most."

"Did you also know that if I can't move on and have a…a…" She was still in shock over seeing herself with a son. How could she tell her husband there was a possibility that she would fall in love with someone else and have a baby? *This future has a forty percent chance of happening.* Malcolm's words kept her from continuing.

There was also a forty percent chance she'd be isolated. She had to find an alternate path.

Cam had floated closer. "What is it, love? What did they show you that you're so afraid of?"

She waved him off. "What they showed me were only forty percent possible scenarios. But Malcolm said that if I didn't move on with my life, as in living for me instead of waiting for your visits, that we wouldn't be allowed to be together after I die. Is that true?"

He floated toward the fireplace. Even in life, that was his thinking spot. But what did he have to think about? He brushed his hair off his forehead. "The truth is, I don't know. Malcolm could be right. Because you're my wife, I'm not privy to the parameters. I'm just trying to help you live a fulfilling life without me. I want us to be together again, but I don't want it to be rushed. You deserve to be happy."

"Cam, I *am* happy. I have the shop and my friends and I get to see you once a year. That's enough."

He shook his head. "No, I don't think it is. I think I may have messed up again. In trying to help you and assuage my own guilt, I may have put our happiness in jeopardy again."

His frustration had him fisting his hands. That had always been a sure sign that a rash decision was next. Frantic to avoid that, she latched on to something else Malcolm said. "Oh, I was going to let Malcolm tell you, but I can. I think it will help."

His gaze, which had clouded over as if his self-loathing had affected his eyes, finally focused on her. "What did Malcolm say?"

"He said that if you hadn't fallen off that rock face on Christmas day, there was a ninety percent chance you would have died anyway within a year." She watched him digest that news. Anything to keep him from beating himself up and making another decision they'd both regret.

Cam's eyes had widened in surprise, but now his brows were lowered. "Did he say how else I would die?"

She shook her head. "Nothing in particular, but you should talk to him. You know, he's a very good spirit guide. Joy and Malcolm work well together. They really didn't need any help from me. Then again, I think Joy had the hots for Malcolm right from the start."

Her ploy worked. Cam was staring at her as if she'd grown whiskers and a tail. "Worked well together? Are we talking about the same Malcolm and Joy? Spirits of Christmas Future?"

She grinned. "Yes. They were like a well-oiled machine. Sometimes he'd make me think about something then she'd make me think about something. They even mixed up taking me to fun and heart-wrenching visits. I tried to blame Malcolm for how I felt about an uncomfortable visit, but as Joy pointed out, it was my decisions in the future that caused it."

Cam's shoulders fell, something she'd never seen happen when he was alive. That in itself worried her. "Isn't that what you wanted?"

He nodded. "Yes, it is."

"Then why do you look so defeated. Is there anything I can do? We work well as a team, too. Look what we've done with six spirits already." She smiled to hide her fear at Cam's concerned look.

"Speaking of spirits, I need to have them debrief. I'm still angry at them for upsetting you so much."

She flounced over to her chair since Mac was still sitting in Cam's and she sat on the arm. "I'm made of strong stuff. Besides, I got to be held by you, so I'm definitely not complaining."

Cam grimaced, which hurt more than she wanted him to know. Had he moved on? Was this odd job he had his new life? Not comfortable with her thought, she pointed to Mac. "For two years, he sat in my chair. Now he's in yours again. He can't seem to make up his mind."

Mac stopped washing himself to look at her, then went back to chewing on his hind claws.

Cam studied the cat. "He's almost seven years old now. I guess he's entitled to change his mind."

She winked. "I think that's a woman's prerogative, not an age thing."

"True." Cam shook his head as if clearing it, then glanced at the clock. "I need to go."

Her heart tightened. "But you'll be back, right? There's still almost three hours before Christmas day. Your spirits work fast."

"I'll make a deal with you. You get dressed and go to Brody's party, and—"

She jumped off the arm of her chair. "Wait a minute. How do you know Brody has a party tonight? Have you been spying on me?"

He chuckled, the first smile she'd seen from him since he brought her home. "No, I don't have to. Brody will always throw a Christmas Eve party. It's just who he is."

She was pleased she'd made him smile. "Fine, I'll go to the party, but I'm coming home by half past eleven at the latest."

"Half past eleven?" His lip quirked up at that. "Since when do Americans say half past?"

"Since this one married a Scot and lives in Deervale, Scotland. I even say 'wee' on occasion."

He laughed again, making her feel oddly better. "I'll see you back here later."

"Will you phase through me?" She loved feeling Cam's essence as he did that. It made her happy again.

"Let's wait until later, okay?"

"As long as you promise."

"I do." He started to float up toward the ceiling.

Holly ran beneath him. "Nice balls."

His laughter filled her heart as he disappeared. Taking a deep breath, she plopped down in her chair, needing a few minutes to relax before changing for the party.

Mac sat up and stared at her.

"Did you need something, Mac?"

The cat yawned, opening his mouth wide before closing it and licking his lips. Then he jumped down and trotted over to his litter box.

At least she didn't have to worry about Mac and she'd cheered up Cam. Now if she could just figure out how to cheer herself up, she'd be in good shape.

~~*~~

Joy sat on the ground in her blue sundress, the standing stone at her back, Malcolm's head resting in her lap. After what appeared to be a day and a half of all types of sex, eating and falling deeper in love with Malcolm, she felt a certain unease.

"What are you thinking about?" Malcolm held her hand against his naked chest.

All she'd done is told him she liked him better in his kilt with no shirt and he hadn't donned one since. That he was so responsive to her still thrilled her. "I'm uncomfortable with all this idle time. We should have heard from Cameron by now."

Malcolm sat up, his hard abs tensing as he lifted himself and turned to face her, crossing his legs in front of him. "I admit to a wee bit of concern myself. I thought he could handle being around his wife, but if he is as weak as she is, he'll be trapped."

"Do you think we should look for him?" She had no idea where besides his office or Holly's home. She didn't even know where his replica home in the afterlife was, though she had no doubt it was the same home Holly lived in.

Malcolm shook his head, his silky black hair falling over his right eyebrow. "Cameron reports to those far above us. Even if we found him, the only help we could offer is what they approve."

"Speaking of that," she looked at him shrewdly. "How did you know we could touch without electric shock after you told me you loved me?"

"It's hard to explain. I saw something in the mist. Two eyes laughing at me. I figured either some entity was playing with me because I enjoy sexcapades, or it was laughing at me for finally falling in love again. As it turns out, it was the second."

"I'm so glad." And she was. He'd shown her so many new things and created feelings she'd never had before. "I've never been so happy while alive or afterwards. There's only one tiny piece that remains open, but I'm not allowed to know that so I'm content."

Malcolm took her hand in his. "You mean your niece?"

At his words, her heart skipped a beat. "Do you know what happened?"

"I do." He looked away for a moment. "I admit when I chose you, I wanted to prove to you that the future was not a good place." He chuckled. "But instead you showed me there was happiness in the future. Still, I didn't want to admit it, so I checked on the future after you transitioned."

Suddenly, she couldn't seem to breathe very deeply. "And?"

"I saw your niece and knew that even if she died I could never tell you."

She squeezed his hand in hers, desperate to know, her eyes already tearing up. "Did she die?"

Malcolm smiled. "No, she didn't. In fact, she married and when she bore her first daughter, she named her Joy."

Happiness like she'd never felt swept through her. "That is the most precious gift anyone has ever given me."

He raised her hand and kissed it. "I'm ashamed at my motivation for finding out, but I'm pleased I can make you happy."

She smiled at him despite how blurry he'd become as tears filled her eyes.

"Ach, I thought I made ye happy." He scooted over next to her and pulled her onto his lap.

"You did. I'm just so happy, I welled up."

He ran his hand under her dress. "Like you did in the wee hours of the night?"

She pulled his hand out. "Yes, though for a totally different reason."

He laughed. "True, but if you let my hand wander, we can try to make you well up again."

"You're insatiable, at least when it comes to sex."

He shrugged. "What else is there?"

"Aren't you curious about what happened after you transitioned?"

He stopped trying to wiggle his hand beneath her dress. "I never was. I figured once 'The Future' was gone from the streets that the vermin simply took over again. But what I've realized since working with you is something far more important."

Now he had her full attention. "What?"

"I always blamed Blair's death on my decision to walk through one of the underground alleyways that night. We could have stayed above on the main road, but I was anxious to get home. Like Cameron, I felt guilty, that I was at fault. But I was wrong."

She could sense him trying to find the right words. The importance of his new understanding obvious. "How so?"

His hand sought hers as if he wanted her to understand, too. "Because of Blair's death, I became judge, jury and executioner for the criminals I caught. I was a one-man force far more powerful than any single Watchman because I was unpredictable and gave no quarter. The weaker vermin scattered and the stronger were whittled down one by one. Glasgow became safer for everyone. When I was killed, I ended up here. That tells me that I was meant to clean up the criminal underground that had developed there."

She held his hand in both of hers. "So, you don't blame yourself for her death anymore?"

He looked her in the eye. "I blame it on fate. When I looked at

Cameron's possible futures and every one of them ended in his early death, I finally saw my own life in a similar perspective. I was meant to clean up the city. I finally looked at Blair's possible futures and if Blair hadn't died that night, she would have died in a similar fashion that would have sent me into the same vigilante rage."

"I see you've come to terms with *your* life. What about me?" Cameron's voice as he floated down to the ground opposite them made her jump.

Still, she was relieved. "I'm so glad you're still with us."

He solidified and sat on the ground with his legs crossed, his kilt falling between his legs. "I'm not that easy to be rid of." He turned his gaze on Malcolm. "So, what about me? You said I was fated to die sometime that year. Was every scenario one where I risked my life for a cheap rush?"

"Yes." Malcolm tone was lower, even more serious. "Because that was who you were. That you had five years with Holly was your bonus. You were able to know true happiness, just as I did and I do now."

Cameron leaned back on his hands. "Except now I must wait for my return to happiness and at this rate, that will never happen."

Concern wormed its way back into her heart. "Why? Won't you and Holly be together again?"

Cameron shoved his hair off his forehead. "Only if I can get her to accept Ethan."

"Oh." She looked at Malcolm. They'd seen her reaction to her own son. It wasn't good. Then again, what if the boy's existence was threatened? There was nothing stronger than a mother's instinct to protect her child. "I think the key to that is her son, but will you be allowed to send more spirits?"

Cameron wouldn't look at them. "I don't know. I had thought she wasn't supposed to know about Ethan, but now I think she was. I'm just not sure how to proceed." He grimaced. "I haven't discussed it yet with my superiors."

Disappointed, she sighed. "So, you don't know yet if Malcolm will be able to continue on as a spirit guide?"

Cameron smiled tiredly. "Yes, I do know that. He won't."

"What?" She scrambled off Malcolm's lap, but he kept her from moving into her superior's space. "You just said we accomplished what needed to be done, and I can attest to the fact that he only did what you wanted."

Cameron frowned. "What are you talking about? He didn't change his methods. He still shocked the living, many times, as a matter of fact."

"But I did, too. You told us not to be subtle."

Cameron stared at her for a moment then broke into a laugh. "Ach, I meant for *you* not to be subtle. Not *him*." Cameron pointed at Malcolm, still chuckling. "That's what I get for trying to help."

She sighed with relief. If he admitted he said it, though he meant something different, then maybe Malcolm could stay. "If you want, we could continue to work as a team."

Cameron rose to his feet, shaking his head. "Not for me. My troubles are still ahead, but you two are done. You've both come to terms with your lives. You no longer need to be spirit guides."

"Done?" How could that be? She hadn't done anything wrong?

Malcolm rose and gave her his hand to help her up. "Aye, Joy. We're done because we have somewhere else we need to be."

She looked from him to Cameron, who was nodding, and back to Malcolm. "We do? Where?"

"Don't ye feel it, lass? The happiness? The contentment? The love?"

She *did* feel it, but it wasn't just from him or inside her. It was everywhere. She looked to where Cameron stood, and he simply waved, half his body no longer visible as warmth and light surrounded her and Malcolm. "What is it?"

He wrapped his arms around her. "It's our future."
She smiled up at him, love filling her heart. "Oh, yes."

Epilogue

Cameron watched as yet another pair of his spirit guides were hidden by white light as they transitioned beyond him. He'd accepted early on when he'd first asked to help Holly that he'd remain behind until she crossed over.

All he wanted was for her to be happy. That would make him happy.

Malcolm's information about his own death had him pondering his next step. He only had one more chance to help Holly, but he shuddered to think of the risk. Even so, he'd do whatever was required of him.

When he'd been told he had to use Malcolm and whoever the man chose as a partner, he'd known it would be rough on Holly, yet she seemed in relatively good spirits. And he'd garnered a lot more information from his spirit guides than he thought he was supposed to. It may just be the edge he needed.

Now, for the first time, he could go to Holly with a clear conscience. When she'd first told him Malcolm's predictions for his death, he wasn't sure if he should believe her because Malcolm was known for exaggerating facts to get the living to change their behavior.

After hearing Malcolm talk about his similar guilt and reiterate what he said, Cameron was much more confident in where he stood.

He walked to the standing stone Joy and Malcolm had been sitting against and slapped it in celebration. The vibration he felt had him placing his hand against it again. No wonder Malcolm had figured it all out. He'd had a direct line to the timeline.

Taking his hand away, Cameron phased and flew upward. The entire valley would disappear into the ether, but he was sure where Joy and Malcolm now were, was far better. Setting his sights on half-past eleven in Deervale, Scotland, Christmas Eve, he sped for Holly's house.

As he hovered above the roof of what had once been *their* home, he couldn't help thinking that it simply wasn't anymore. It was *hers,* and she needed to see that as well. Floating down through the ceiling, he found only Mac in the living room. He glanced at the clock to see he was right on time.

Was Holly still at Brody's? Did that mean she was having a good time? Even as his chest filled with hope, his disappointment caught him off guard.

Shit, it appeared Holly wasn't the only one having a hard time letting go. He should be hoping that Holly didn't get home before midnight, but instead he found himself watching the clock.

And Mac was watching him…intently. He floated over to the gray beast and stared in to its golden eyes. "Are you taking care of Holly for me?" He scratched the cat under the chin. "I'm counting on you to keep her company. Make her feel loved. Keep her safe. All the things I did. It's all on your shoulders, so it's worth your while to help me show her she can move on."

The cat began to purr and the next thing he knew he was stroking the furry critter's back and tail. He'd rather be stroking Holly, but that couldn't happen.

She was as beautiful inside as outside. How would he ever let her go? Coco had said they were soulmates. That had to mean they would remain connected somehow. "Ouch."

He pulled his hand away from the cat. "You bit me. Since when do you bite people?"

The doorknob turning on the front door had him forgetting the cat. Holly walked in wearing a forest-green sweater with white snowflakes and a green corduroy flare skirt. Her hair was pulled back by a white headband with green snowflakes, and she carried a paper sack.

Setting the bag on the floor, she dropped her keys on the table at the side door and noticed him in the mirror. "Cam!" She spun around. "You're here already." She looked past him. "Oh, no! Brody's clock must be slow. I thought I still had another five minutes."

"It's okay, love. Do what you need to do."

"I don't need to do anything." She walked over to where he stood near his old chair. "It's weird. I feel like I should be able to kiss you hello."

He floated closer to the tree, away from her, not wanting her to keep thinking that way. "How was the party?"

She came to stand near him. "It was nice. Sarah confided in me that she and Brody are going to try for a baby. I didn't say a word about what was in store for them."

"That's my girl."

She took a deep breath. "Ethan was there."

"And did you talk to him like the old friend he is?" Cameron's gut tightened.

"I tried. It's a little hard because I've been avoiding him and I know how he feels about me, but…"

"But what, hen. You can tell me." He barely kept from reaching for her to pull her close, which would only frustrate him more, since he couldn't. Luckily, the cat jumped down and started rubbing against his legs, distracting him.

"I finally accepted his invitation to Christmas dinner tomorrow. It will be at his parents' home here in town, so that should keep it at a nice friendship level."

"I'm proud of you. I know it's not easy, but I think the more time you spend with people you really care about, the easier it will be." He stepped away from Mac, who started to paw at his bare knee.

"Wait a minute." She ran back to the bag and pulled out a box. "Look what I got in the gift exchange. It's a music box and you'll never believe what it plays."

He smiled, thrilled to see her feeling happy about something.

"Listen." She opened the box and he listened, but he didn't recognize it.

"What is it?"

She closed the lid and looked at him. "Don't you remember that Christmas Eve we spent back in New Hampshire and the radio kept playing this over and over?"

He really didn't remember that. As he tried to think of being in New Hampshire, he couldn't bring to mind anything from there. Only Holly. He had to get to work fast on her next Christmas or he might lose all their memories before he had her future solidified.

Only by having her set on her future could he be assured he would keep her forever. How ironic that he had to give her away to keep her. "For some reason I thought it was a different song."

"Oh, you were always getting *God Rest Ye Marry Gentlemen* mixed up with *Deck the Halls*. That must be why you didn't remember." She put the music box back in the bag. "This year, they had the usual games, lots to eat and drink, and someone brought their cousin from America, so I was able to chat about home a bit."

That she was so animated about the party pleased him. "Do you think your mom and John will come over this year for another visit?"

"I hope so. I'm going to ask them. I'm already planning to see them and the Tinders in January." She paused. "It's so nice to talk to you about everyday things. I really wish we could see each other more often."

"I know you do, love." *More than you know.* "You'll just have to make a couple of very close friends so you can do that with them. I'm going to come back next year, but it may be a very short visit and possibly my last one."

Her face went white at his statement. "Your last one? Why?"

He shook his head. "My presence in your life isn't helping you anymore. Now, it's hurting you." His own heart ached at the thought of not letting her see him, but at least he could check on her when he wanted.

"Cam, you're not hurting me at all, and we know you don't need to feel guilty anymore."

He gave her a soft smile. "I do know that now, thanks to you. That's very important for me as that will help me move on. You need to, too. Malcolm was right. If we want forever together, we need to say goodbye. But not this year, okay?"

She nodded, though he could see the sheen of tears in her eyes.

"I want you to focus on just a few people and maybe even look at a big change in your life in the future. Can you do that for me?"

"I can." She stepped closer to him, but looked at the tiny bell ornament on the tree that marked their wedding day. "What should I do about Ethan?"

He lifted his arms to embrace her and stopped, scratching behind his head instead. "Be the good friend to him you've always been. That's all I ask."

Her smile was more confident now. "I can do that."

"Good." He glanced at the clock. "I have to leave now."

"I understand. But don't forget to phase through me. That feeling lasts a whole day and it's Christmas day in just two minutes."

"I couldn't forget that." He smiled, showing her with his eyes the love he still had for her. "Merry Christmas, hen."

"Merry Christmas, Cam."

When she closed her eyes, he phased through her, feeling her very essence tangle with his own before he continued out the front of the building, her scent and sweetness residing inside him.

It was a very selfish feeling and one he'd need to make do without soon, but it was necessary. He just hoped he could help her as much as he needed to when he was only granted fifteen minutes of living time each time he saw her.

Rising upward, he flew over to Ethan's parents' home where Ethan always stayed Christmas Eve night. He found Ethan asleep in the parlor, Christmas carols playing. He'd been reading by the light of the tree, a book open on his lap.

Cameron floated over to his old friend, a sharp pain hitting his heart at how much he missed him. "I'm counting on you, my friend. Don't let me down."

Ethan's breathing remained normal as expected. Cameron bent over to see which book his friend had chosen for Christmas Eve. "A Christmas Carol by Charles Dickens."

He laughed. "If only it were really that simple."

Leaving the homey atmosphere, he sped outside and into the ether, anxious now to strike the next deal with his bosses and finally give Holly her second chance at love.

For updates, sneak peeks, and special prizes, sign up to receive the latest news from Lexi at http://bit.ly/LexiUpdate

Read on for a sneak peek of One of a Kind Christmas (A
Christmas Carol: Book 4)

CHAPTER ONE

Why was he awake?

Ethan Stewart listened, keeping his eyes closed, his body and
mind alert. Something had woken him from his dream of walking by
Loudoun Castle with Holly Douglas.

Despite the fact that all was silent except for the usual screech
of the tawny owl outside, he still didn't doubt his senses. Years of
ancient Scottish martial arts study had tuned him in to his own sixth
sense.

Slowly, he opened his eyes. His room remained dark. The heavy
damask curtains on his floor-to-ceiling windows were closed except
for a sliver of moonlight that sliced across the floor.

His bedroom was on the second story of his family's ancestral
home, and he doubted anyone could get in without making a noise,
but it was still a possibility. Could it be an animal had scurried in
while the front door was open earlier in the day and finally made it
up to his room?

Unfortunately, his bed was too high for him to see the floor
from where he lay, so there was no help for it but to sit up. Taking a
deep breath in case something attacked, he rose in one fluid motion,
sending his feet over the side of the bed to land on the floor, his
knees bent slightly, his hands ready.

He scanned his room but there were areas in total blackness
that his gaze couldn't penetrate. "Who's there?" It was a stupid

question, but he asked it anyway. His voice could very well scare a critter into revealing its whereabouts with noise.

"Just an old friend."

Ethan's blood chilled. He hadn't heard that voice in almost four years, but he'd never forget it. "Cameron?"

"Aye."

Ethan turned toward the far corner of his room. He had to be dreaming. Despite the lack of sound, he sensed movement just before the spirit of Cameron Douglas floated out of the darkness and into the sliver of moonlight.

Dressed in his dark green, black and white tartan kilt, black sleeveless t-shirt and black army boots, the spirit's hazel eyes appeared a murky grey and no smile lifted his lips like it had so often in life.

He wasn't dreaming. The man hovering a meter off the floor looked exactly like his best friend, only he wasn't solid, more like a hologram. Immediately, guilt tightened his stomach. Had his interest in the man's widow somehow called him from his grave?

Refusing to jump to conclusions, he relaxed his stance. "How can you be here?"

His friend floated to the floor, but otherwise remained where he was. "It's time to tell you."

A Christmas Carol Series:

Pleasures of Christmas Past
Desires of Christmas Present
Temptations of Christmas Future
One of a Kind Christmas

Read on for an excerpt from Christmas with Angel (Last Chance
Series: Book 1)

CHAPTER ONE

Last Chance Ranch, Arizona December 23rd

Cole Hatcher added two pillows to the makeshift bed of
sleeping bags on the hay. He'd unzipped each and spread them out
so he and Lacey could crawl in together. Maybe if they could have a
little privacy, they could settle their Christmas issue.

He'd pilfered all the snowflake decorations from the tree inside
and hung them from the beams. In his mind, he'd envisioned it to
look like it was snowing, but in reality, it looked like plastic, glass and
felt snowflakes hanging from beams. Lacey would get it though. She
couldn't expect more than this from her cowboy.

Adjusting the garland around the stall walls, he pulled over
the small table he used for grooming the horses and placed it next
to the bed. With a rag he'd grabbed from the house, he wiped it
off and placed a bottle of wine on it with two plastic cups. "That
should do it." His Christmas Eve present was ready, though a few
hours early.

Stuffing the rag in his back pocket, he turned the battery-
operated lantern to low and set it next to the wine. "Perfect."

As he headed out of the barn, the six horses in residence paid
him no heed except for Angel. Her wary eyes watched him until he
was out of sight.

Giving Angel to Lacey had been the best thing he'd done for that horse, besides take her from her owner. She was so fearful of men that her bond with Lacey had grown strong.

Now if he could just get his fiancé onto the same page with him, life would be great again.

Cole strode across the dirt yard, the only sound to break the crisp night air, the two note call of a whippoorwill. The quiet beckoned him, but he needed Lacey to truly enjoy it. The house lights should have been welcoming but with his two cousins in residence, one baby, Billy and his grandparents, the four bedroom house was packed.

He took the stairs to the porch two at a time. Pulling back the screen door, he opened the heavy, ironwood front door. As he stepped in, he had to stop himself from stepping back out.

The baby cried upstairs while his two cousins, Logan and Trace argued. A door slammed on the upper level then Trace stomped down the stairs, yelling back over his shoulder, "I'll be watching the game with Grandpa if you come to your senses!" He nodded to Cole as he passed by.

Old Billy, who used to work and live at Poker Flat and had just spent two months in rehab for alcoholism, ambled through the front hall from the kitchen, a bottle of water in his hand and a smile on his face. The television in the living room clicked on just as Billy entered and the volume increased substantially.

Cole winced, the noise level and activity in the house was almost painful. Like Lacey, he couldn't wait for their own home to be completed, but it barely had walls and was far too incomplete for them to have the privacy and quiet they needed. Since Lacey had given up her casita at the Poker Flat Nudist Resort, they had nowhere to go…except the barn.

She was probably in their room where she always retreated right after dinner to crunch numbers, do research, or iron clothes for work. He ran up the stairs, excited to show her the present he'd arranged, and opened the door to the bedroom.

Lacey stood next to the bed, her deep pink sweater fitting her like a second-skin, wisps of blonde hair escaping her long braid. Her maroon skirt flowed about her, accentuating her delicate femininity. He still couldn't believe this hot woman was his. She had a basket of laundry dumped out on their bed, clean clothes strewn over the quilt and a small pile folded to her right. He walked straight to her and wrapped his arms around her waist from behind. "I have a surprise for you."

She stilled then sighed. "Is it ear plugs?"

He kissed her neck beneath her ear, loving how tiny she felt against him. "Even better."

She dropped his fire department t-shirt and turned in his arms. "Better is good." She lifted her arms around his neck. "Don't get me wrong. I love your family. There just seems to be so many of them in this particular house. And now that Billy's here, it makes it very cramped."

He looked into her light brown eyes that reminded him of amaretto. "You love my family? Even my parents?"

She lowered her lashes and stared at his chest.

Damn, he needed to wait to discuss that. Talking about his parents only brought up what his mother had done to break them apart. That didn't set the mood he wanted. He wouldn't press it now. "So aren't you a little bit curious about my surprise?"

She lifted her gaze to meet his. "Is this my Christmas Eve present?"

His family had always exchanged gifts on Christmas day, but maybe he and Lacey could start their own tradition. "Yes, just a few hours early."

She looked over her shoulder at the clock sitting on the nightstand. "Only three hours and seventeen minutes early. Should I wait?"

He started to grin but it turned to a grimace as his cousin's baby let out an ear-piercing wail. "You might be able to, but I can't."

At the sound of the baby's scream, Lacey buried her head against his chest. She lifted it to look up at him. "I could use a surprise right about now."

"Good." He kissed her on the forehead then let her go so he could take her hand. As he took a step toward the door, she resisted. "I thought you were going to give me a surprise."

"We have to go outside for this."

She pointed to the pile of clothes. "But I need to finish folding the laundry."

"Leave them. This is more important."

"Okay." She let him pull her down the hall.

When they got to the top of the stairs, he released her hand and stepped aside so she could descend first. Another screeching wail sounded from above, and they both picked up their pace. As he opened the front door, the television volume increased another decimal in the living room and from the corner of his eye he caught sight of Billy who had joined his grandfather and Trace.

Lacey stepped onto the porch and sighed.

No sooner had he closed the door than she placed her hand on his chest. "Do you hear that?"

He listened. The quiet was almost deafening until four hoots, sounding like a bouncing ball, broke the silence. "You mean the Screech Owl?"

She smiled slyly. "No, I mean the quiet."

He grinned. "Wait until you see my surprise." He took her hand and they walked down the steps toward the barn.

"I hope you didn't get me another horse. I'm very attached to Angel and I think she'd get jealous."

He shook his head. "No, it's not a horse. Luckily, I haven't had any calls this week. Maybe the Christmas spirit has people being kinder to their animals." He frowned at the thought of what else the Christmas season brought. "Now if we could just get Christmas tree fires under control, everyone could have a happy Christmas."

She squeezed his hand. "I've never understood the need for a live evergreen tree in the Arizona desert. It's so dry. If a person wants to smell evergreens, they can always go up to Prescott for the day or take a hike right here in our own mountains."

"You make the house smell great with those scented candles you use. I'm glad you found them in the glass jars."

She stopped at the entrance to the barn and looked at him. "Can you turn off the firefighter tonight and give me the cowboy who loves to save abused, hurt, and unwanted horses?"

He grinned sheepishly. "I'll try. Actually, your surprise is definitely from the cowboy." He winked.

Lacey's gaze roamed over him, and he couldn't help but count himself lucky all over again. To have found her a second time, at a fire no less, had been sheer luck. That she was just as dedicated to his horse rescue ranch as he was, was a bonus. Her wizardry with the finances had also improved their solvency. But to have captured her heart once more against all odds was the greatest luck of all. "If you keep looking at me like that, your surprise might have to wait."

She widened her eyes. "Like what?" She even batted her lashes.

He laughed and pulled her into his embrace. "I love you, soon-to-be Lacey Hatcher."

"I know." She stood on tiptoe to give him a kiss.

When she didn't deepen the kiss, he had to stop himself from lowering his lips to hers again. The open barn door was not the place to start making love to his woman. Reluctantly, he released her, but grasped her hand again.

After pulling the large door closed behind him, he led Lacey through the barn, passing the filled stalls until she slowed by Angel.

He understood and let go, continuing toward the last stall, not wanting to disturb the bond between her and the rescued horse.

No sooner had Lacey turned toward the white Arabian, than Angel gave a soft nicker and walked to the stall door. Lacey pet the badly marred head, cooing to her like one would talk with a baby.

Cole never tired of watching their connection. He had almost given up hope that Angel would ever interact with humans again after the abuse she'd take from her former owner. That the horse came into his life shortly after he had found Lacey again made him think it was fate. Though the horse shied away from men, she completely trusted Lacey.

When Lacey finished, she walked slowly toward him, or was she sauntering toward him? Shit, his muscles tensed in anticipation.

She still wore her clothes from work, her long skirt swishing against her white cowboy boots. The sweater showed off her figure even if it didn't reveal even a hint of cleavage. It was hard to believe she worked at a nudist resort. He was thankful once again that the resort had a strict policy about employees keeping their clothes on during work. He would go insane if Lacey was supposed to work nude. On the other hand, because Kendra owned the nudist resort she was expected to be nude. He had no idea how Wade handled his fiancé being naked half the day. Cole couldn't do it.

But Lacey was sexy even with her clothes on, especially after a long day, when her braid had loosened and her messy wheat-colored hair made it look as if she'd just spent an hour in bed with him.

He watched her eyes closely as she approached. Her gaze was riveted to him and his chest puffed with pride. When she licked her lips, he had to force himself to stay still as every tendon pushed at him to move.

Finally, her gaze flitted to the stall behind him and her lips formed a pleased smile. "Oh Cole, it's the best present you could have given me."

He released the breath he'd been holding and opened his arms. "You like it?"

She walked straight into his embrace. "I love it."

"It might get a little chilly tonight."

She shrugged. "That's why I have you to keep me warm."

"Just to keep you warm?" He frowned. "I was hoping to start a fire inside you."

Lacey's short intake of breath had his cock taking notice.

She wrapped her arms around his neck. "You are as good at starting fires as putting them out."

"Only for you." He lowered his head and kissed her.

She pressed her body against him and pushed her tongue between his lips. He caught it with his own.

Every nook of her mouth was like new territory. He tasted the tartness of the wine she had with dinner and a flavor that was all Lacey. His hands roamed over her back, feeling her sweater slide against silk.

His cock hardened at the thought of what his Racy Lacey might be wearing underneath.

She pulled her lips away abruptly. "You have too many clothes on."

"I was thinking the same about you." He wiggled his brow. "I bet I can take my shirt off faster than you can." He let his arm go slack in anticipation of the race. They were always betting about sex.

She kept her arms around him. "And what does the winner get?"

"I'm thinking, choice of position." At his words, a shiver ran through her body, sending lightning straight to his balls.

"On the count of three. One. Two. Three."

No sooner had she dropped her arms than he reached back and pulled his flannel over his head. One button pinged across the stall, hitting the wood, as his face cleared the tail of the shirt.

Lacey had brought the sweater up over her head, but her face was still hidden.

Cole stared at the pale pink corset that cupped her breasts and accentuated her waist and hips. With her skirt still on, she looked like a saloon girl from the old west.

As she pulled the sweater free, she took a breath and her areolas peeked above their confines.

He swallowed hard.

"Are you admiring my new corset?" She smiled slyly, the vixen.

He shook his head as he traced a finger along the top edge of the satiny lingerie. "No, I'm admiring this." He pushed his finger inside the cup and flicked at the hard nipple beneath."

"But you like it, right?"

"I think it might require a closer inspection." He used his other hand to burrow beneath her other cup and lift the breast above the soft satin so the corset held it up for him to view her rosy tip. "Hmm, I'm liking it more and more." He performed the same readjustment on her other breast then stood back. "Now that's perfect." He stared at her hard nipples held aloft. "I really like it."

"I'm glad." Her lips formed a seductive pout. "But I lost the bet."

He reached out one hand and brushed his fingertips across her hard nipples. "Yes, you did."

Her chest rose as she sucked in a breath at his touch.

He loved how responsive she was. "I think it's time you took off your skirt so I can decide exactly what position I want you in."

She cocked her head. "And that must be determined by what I'm wearing underneath my skirt?"

He nodded. His soon-to-be wife never failed to surprise him when they crawled into bed at night. Her love of lingerie had him anticipating their alone time even during dinner. He was definitely the beneficiary of that little fetish. It didn't take much to get Lacey hot, but in the house, she had to keep quiet when they made love, and that took something away from the experience for her. Tonight, she could let go completely with no one the wiser.

Lacey untied the bow at her waist and pushed the skirt down to the barn floor before stepping out of it.

He was too distracted by the movement of her breasts at first, to understand her smile.

"So what position would you like?" Her voice was teasing, a sound he hadn't heard in over a month.

This had definitely been needed. He lowered his gaze and raised his brows. "I can't decide until you take off that damn slip too."

She giggled, another sound he hadn't heard in a while. He needed to do something about that. The stress of building a house, working, caring for the horses with so much family around was too stressful for the only-child Lacey.

As she shimmied out of her slip, his jaw dropped and his cock hardened.

Also by Lexi Post

Paranormal Romance

Masque

Passion's Poison

Passion of Sleepy Hollow

Heart of Frankenstein

Pleasures of Christmas Past (A Christmas Carol Series: Book 1)

Desires of Christmas Present (A Christmas Carol Series: Book 2)

Temptations of Christmas Future (A Christmas Carol Series: Book 3)

One of a Kind Christmas (A Christmas Carol Series: Book 4) Coming 2018

On Highland Time (Time Weavers Inc. Series: Book 1) Coming 2018

Sci-fi Romance

Cruise into Eden (The Eden Series: Book 1)

Unexpected Eden (The Eden Series: Book 2)

Eden Discovered (The Eden Series: Book 3)

Eden Revealed (The Eden Series: Book 4)

Avenging Eden (The Eden Series: Book 5) Coming 2018

Contemporary Cowboy Romance

Cowboys Never Fold (Poker Flat Series: Book 1)

Cowboy's Match (Poker Flat Series: Book 2)

Cowboy's Best Shot (Poker Flat Series: Book 3)
Cowboy's Break (a Poker Flat novella)

Christmas with Angel (Poker Flat Series Book: 2.5/Last Chance Series: Book 1)
Trace's Trouble (Last Chance Series: Book 2)
Fletcher's Flame (Last Chance Series: Book 3)
Logan's Luck: (Last Chance Series: Book 4)
Dillon's Dare (Last Chance Series: Book 5) Coming 2018

Military Romance

When Love Chimes (Broken Valor Series: Book 1)
Poisoned Honor (Broken Valor Series: Book 2)

About Lexi Post

Lexi Post is a New York Times and USA Today best-selling author of romance inspired by the classics. She spent years in higher education taking and teaching courses about the classical literature she loved. From Edgar Allan Poe's short story "The Masque of the Red Death" to Tolstoy's *War and Peace*, she's read, studied, and taught wonderful classics.

But Lexi's first love is romance novels. In an effort to marry her two first loves, she started writing romance inspired by the classics and found she loved it. From hot paranormals to sizzling cowboys to hunks from out of this world, Lexi provides a sensuous experience with a "whole lotta story."

Lexi is living her own happily ever after with her husband and her cat in Florida. She makes her own ice cream every weekend, loves bright colors, and you will never see her without a hat.

www.lexipostbooks.com

www.ingramcontent.com/pod-product-compliance
Lightning Source LLC
Chambersburg PA
CBHW070948120726
47910CB00004B/1164